Those Luck

By A.

Those Lucky Fellas: Part 1

Those Lucky Fellas

Awais Khan

Published by A. A. Khan, 2023.

This is a work of fiction. Similarities to real people, places, or events are entirely coincidental.

THOSE LUCKY FELLAS: PART 1

First edition. August 28, 2023.

ISBN: 979-8223103851

Written by Awais Khan.

Reality is nothing but an illusion springing from one's perception of this world.

Prologue

Lone Star

The senile rowing boat crawled over the calm sea and crept onto the shore of a thin beach. Its weary frame grounded itself upon the narrow strip of dull sand.

Stained with blood, an aging figure rose from within and hopped into the water, tugging on a rope. He toppled onto his weak knees, dropping his empty double-barreled shotgun by his side and glared at his filthy, bruised hands.

It was silent before the determined stranger stood and strolled through the sand, heading toward a pebbled path, marking heavy footprints across the terrain.

The rain began to clout the dirt around him and seep through his bloodied clothes as he journeyed into the nearby soundless woods.

Thirty years had rolled by.

Chapter One

Brave New World

"You can't be serious, Boss," said Benny, worriedly, brushing his dark gray hair through his fingers.

"'Bout what?" Al replied, watching the setting sun paint an orange canvas across the icy sky.

"We ain't comin' out of retirement for... *that* kind of work, Mister King. The Lost Dogs... *we* left that life behind," Benny put forth, ogling the old figure who was almost two decades older than him.

"Look, Benny, we ain't got much of a choice. Do you *really* think I wanna do this, son?" uttered Al and his voice echoed through the valley. "It ain't my fault those bastards can't behave like civilized men! Money has taken over their tiny minds. If they're too blind to see their own greed, then we gotta show it to 'em, make 'em realize they shouldn't have crossed us!"

He adjusted his leather eyepatch and pointed at Benny, spitting his words.

"Wait out here for the rest, Mister Falcon, then you can be on your way. I'm countin' on you five."

"Understood, Al," Benny groaned, tightly closing his eyes.

Slowly, the old man pivoted and hiked through the dusty path leading toward the cream-colored manor. Not a single word was spilled as he journeyed to their cozy home.

As the setting February sun crept farther behind a row of tall pine trees, Benny stood patiently at the edge of a small cliff, glaring at his silver pocket watch before adjusting his dark red tie.

"Goddamnit," he whispered to himself. He revealed a vanilla cigar and gripped it tightly between his teeth, torching it with his engraved lighter. The strong flavor filled his mouth before he blew out the heavy smoke into the cold air.

The wind had been biting the shaved sides and back of his head, but his friendly mutton chops kept his face relatively warm. He held the burning cigar in his mouth and tenderly wiped his circular, silver-rimmed glasses onto his black suit, clearing any dirt and smudges.

When the sun set farther, the lustrous light had shunned onto his light brown eyes, causing them to glow and the terrain around him turned dark blue, burying the island into darkness.

"Nineteen-fifty-one and we *still* ain't retired," mumbled Benny, standing beside his '51 Hudson Hornet and gazing upon its elegant black paint.

Cautiously, he removed the almost-finished cigar from his mouth, bent down and crushed it against the frosty ground before standing erect again and blowing out the heavy smoke.

Soon, after resting his mind on the calm sea, a slow stampede of footsteps emerged from behind him, approaching from the manor.

Benny turned and said, "Gentlemen, it's time. I hope you're all ready."

The group was made up of four men, somewhat in the forties, and they marched toward Benny, bobbing their heads in his direction, carrying heavy firearms and cradling them in their arms. Just like Benny, they donned black suits and red ties and were well-groomed, too.

"Evenin', Boss," said Houston Alfrey, grumpily, before sitting snuggly into the front passenger seat.

THOSE LUCKY FELLAS: PART 1

"Boss, you *sure* this is a good plan?" asked Desmond Kane, charily, opening the black heavy door.

"We gotta do this job either way," Carson Montgomery interrupted, forcibly, who was the tallest from the rest.

"Don't mind them, Boss," Reese August, the shortest, added.

Benny closed his eyes and sighed, "Just get in the car, fellas."

With that, the men carefully rested in the Hudson Hornet and Benny perched behind the wheel, rubbing his hands together.

"What's with the sulkin'?" Houston asked.

"You're one to talk," said Benny, looking over at him and chortling.

"We're crazy to be doing this at night," Desmond mentioned, swaying his head.

"You worry too much, you know that?" Benny responded, looking over his shoulder.

The engine was alive once Benny turned the silver key, and the car rolled over the dirty road, heading out of the towering, black iron gates at the end of the yard.

"You know where we're goin', right?" Carson inquired.

"Of course," Benny replied. "Well, let's hope I remember," he added before tightly grabbing the leather steering wheel.

"Now that I think about it, we never really worked at sundown," Reese voiced.

"We shouldn't really be workin' at all!" supposed Benny, raising his right hand. "Al still wants us paintin' houses. You can never please that man, can ya?"

By now, the sun had faded completely, and darkness had blanketed the sky and the roads. The tires rolled heavily, running from the dusty path onto the cold, frozen asphalt. Benny projected his eyes into the rear-view mirror and back onto the gloomy road ahead.

"Listen to me, gentlemen. We're doin' this job fast. Don't need no attention, 'specially from those Peacekeeper bastards."

When saying those final words, Benny's eyebrows became tense, displaying anger.

"You know, I always thought that by now someone would've rid them from Knox," explained Carson.

Everyone was quiet until Reese theorized. "Thing is, we'll have more shit to deal with if they get involved in our work and I thought we're not doin' work like this no more."

"Well, if you want somethin' done right, you do it yourself," Houston suggested. "That's why we're goin' out tonight."

"We haven't done *this* kind of work in a while," Desmond added.

"Enough! We all know what to do!" yelled Benny, raising his right hand up then back down, clenching the wheel again. "Anyway, the Peacekeepers don't come to the west of Knox very often. We *should* be safe."

As the night began to awaken, the road ahead became darker, with only the car's headlights giving way through the mucky, damp roads. Despite the moon creating rays of light, the clouds spread across the sky, shielding out most of the moonlight.

Benny eased off the gas pedal, and took a left through some more charming country roads, scattered with rolling hills and taller pine trees, along with the dry scent of mud.

"I trust you fellas to do a good job tonight. You won't let me down, will ya?" Benny put forth, observing the men through the mirror.

They all looked at him blankly.

"I'm kiddin'. We're a *little* rusty, but I *know* we still got it. We've been workin' together for many years and we ain't dead yet, so let's keep it that way," he declared.

They all chuckled.

"What's so funny? I *am* serious," he said, smirking, and drove cautiously up a steep hill. "It just don't feel right, though. We shouldn't be doin' this. It don't... *feel* like it used to."

Benny drove with his right hand lounging on the wheel, and his left hand adjusted his spectacles.

Overhead, the clouds began to open, like a rock causing a pond to ripple, allowing the moonlight to gleam onto the road.

"We're almost there, gentlemen," he advised the rest.

A few trucks would pass by, carrying goods and, with that, some pickup trucks, too, usually transporting fruit, vegetables and hay for the farms and local stores. A giant lake was in view to the right side of their car, lit by lanterns spreading across its dock. In the center of the lake sat a white boat with two men throwing a fishing net overboard.

Desmond stared in bewilderment and said, "They ain't fishing right."

"The hell you know about fishin'?" replied Carson.

Houston smiled, turned his head and asked, "Tell us, Carson, you ever caught a fish in your life?"

"Yes, I have," he smirked and bobbed his head at him. "It ain't difficult, man."

"Nobody can fish as good as me," Reese included.

Benny chuckled.

"You know, sometimes I wonder where Mister King found

you fools. Seems unfortunate," he said, joyfully, and released a sigh.

After driving for almost twenty minutes, they approached a little grungy wooden cabin resting upon a hillside near a deep cave.

"We made it," announced Benny.

Chapter Two

Looking For a Four-Leaf Clover

Arriving at the cabin, Benny parked his black Hudson Hornet alongside a wooden barrel that was slightly damaged and stained by the rain. A few rusty, dull tools remained beside an empty barrel, and some tools scattered the floor, and the cramped cabin itself had seen better days; its roof needed the stone tiles replacing, its wooden walls were cracked and the makeshift rope handle to the front door seemed to be smothered in grease. A forty-eight-star American flag situated on its roof, waving gently in the chilly wind.

Leaving the car discreetly, they stood on the path outside of the hideous cabin, rifles and submachine guns in hand, and Benny had something similar. He excluded himself by walking to the trunk of the car, lifting the heavy metal and revealing a firearm from underneath a long blanket. It was a pristine Browning Automatic Rifle.

The firearms shimmered under the moonlit night sky.

"You still using that?" Carson asked politely.

"Why wouldn't I? It still works, like it's brand new. Packs a strong punch and it ain't too heavy," he acknowledged, pointing at his prized possession and walking toward the gloomy cabin.

Benny looked over his shoulder, then back at the door.

"Let's do this," he whispered.

Forcefully, with his left hand, he snapped the cabin's door open with the gun gripped in his right hand and its stock sunk into his shoulder.

There were dirty miners, maybe two or three, sitting at a decrepit table in the center of the main room, which had a thick, sweaty odor. As the gang entered the cabin, the miners jerked up in dismay.

"Hello, gentlemen," Benny began. "How are we doin' this *fine* evenin'?"

One miner, covered in dirt, stared at Benny and began hurling Spanish words, all while the rest of Benny's crew lowered their guns when entering the cabin. Although Benny was miffed, he lowered his gun, too.

"Goddammit," he hushed to himself, with his left thumb and index finger rubbing his eyes, as if he was trying to dismiss a headache.

Turning around to his own men, Benny gawked, then turned around again, this time facing the miners.

"All right, well," Carson began, "someone's gotta make 'em talk."

Carson and Houston walked to the other side of the mucky cabin, now standing behind the poor workers, who were studying the strangers that had just barged through their door; looking anxious.

"They don't look so dangerous to me, Boss," said Desmond, standing beside Benny.

"You sure we're in the right place?" said Houston, surprised.

Reese began creeping gently across the room, analyzing the bland furniture.

"Don't be seein' much here. They're not even a threat to us," he interpreted.

Suddenly, another rusty door in the corner of the cabin

burst open, revealing a dark-skinned man wielding a pistol, aiming it directly at Benny, then turning it toward the other men.

Swiftly, Benny and the gang raised their weapons at the only threat in the room before he yelled, "Hey! You don't want to be doin' that, amigo!"

He supposed that someone would be shot, but who?

The Spanish-speaking man jumped up, holding his dirty hands out toward both sides of the main room, and began yelling.

Calmly, everyone had lowered their weapons, still glaring at the miner with the pistol.

Pointing, Benny asked the strange man his name. "*You.* Name."

"Me?" he asked politely. "Diego," he answered.

"Good! Pleasure to meet you, Diego," said Benny, sulkily. "Speak English?" he asked again, causing Diego to nod his head in disagreement.

Turning to the other miners, he asked again, but yelled, "Anyone in this damn room speak English?"

The man who barged in earlier raised his hand. "I do. My name is Donato."

"Welcome aboard," Benny countered.

As they all sat stiff around the dry benches, they placed their firearms slowly against the unpolished table. Diego and the other miners had sat down, too.

Resting upon an iron shelf was an old radio. What was it playing?

It was too quiet to make out.

A paltry lantern was hung against the door, with its flame

slowly dying. To illuminate the rest of the cabin, there were smaller white candles placed on the tables and drawers near the beds. Three miniature candles were placed on the main table; one on each end and one in the center, creating an orange, warm atmosphere.

The door behind them creaked, allowing Donato to walk through, carrying a few iron mugs and two glass jars of moonshine. He planted them onto the table, in front of his *guests*, so to speak.

Benny dragged the mug to place it in front of himself and lifted the glass jar to pour in the moonshine; about a quarter of a cup to capture a little taste. Desmond grabbed the jar and poured it into another mug, too, before handing it over to Houston, who did the same. Meanwhile, Carson and Reese were taking turns flooding their mugs.

Gently, Benny raised his iron mug to his nose and took a sniff. He took a sip. It had a thin texture that dissolved in his mouth, but the liquid stung his tongue.

"Jeez, what is that?" he shrieked.

"Spanish recipe, amigo," Diego said, smiling at Benny.

"You Spanish folk are crazy. If you were as strong as your moonshine, we wouldn't have to be here."

They all laughed.

Reese took a sip. "It's all right."

Then Desmond had a taste. "Oh, lord, this ain't good stuff."

Carson placed his mug down after taking in the scent. "I ain't trying that. Not to be rude, amigos, but maybe another time."

Finally, Houston's turn was next. He took a few tiny drops to his tongue and moved it around his mouth, then began coughing. After a brief moment, he coughed and said, "It ain't *half* bad."

Donato's open-mouthed smile turned into a laugh. "Americanos, *this* is alcohol!" he expressed.

For a brief moment, a strong silence filled the room.

"Anyway, sorry about the intrusion earlier. I thought you people were the ones we was after," Benny began, placing his mug onto the tabletop. "But back to it. You called Mister King a couple hours ago? You boys wanted our help?"

"You're The Lost Dogs, right?" Donato asked, straightening his back.

"Who'd you think we were?" replied Benny, staring at his face. "Looks like you ran into some trouble earlier. Tell us what happened."

"Mister King said you'd come."

"And here we are... to help, obviously," said Benny, sulkily. "Now, start talkin'. We ain't got all night."

Donato expressed, "There's this rich family. The Comstock family, only a few miles away from *this* cabin. They heard a rumor that we were making moonshine."

"Go on," Benny suggested, raising his chin.

"When they arrived a couple days ago, they asked us to make them a few jars of moonshine, but we refused, as the price was far too low," Donato continued, seeming upset.

"Then what?" asked Houston.

"Comstock sent men to threaten us, knowing full well that we mined for gold in this region. When they realized the gold was for The Lost Dogs, they took it and told us to keep our mouths shut."

"You shittin' us?" Carson questioned.

"All true," Donato stated; his eyes became watery. "We had no other choice but to hand it over."

After the room had quietened down a little, Reese began speaking. "So much for keepin' quiet. Where do these bastards live?"

There was no response from the miners.

"Please, amigos," Desmond said, leaning forward to reassure these poor men.

Donato coughed and sat up. "Follow the road back where you came and take a left. Go straight until you come across Honeyspoon Farms. Keep following the main road up the hills and you will arrive at the Comstock farmhouse."

Immediately, Benny stood up, followed by the rest of his men, and headed toward the front door, guns in hand.

Desperately, Donato stood up and chased them, yelling, "Please, whatever you do, never say we sent you!"

Benny turned around, "Oh, you don't worry about nothin'. They'll never threaten you again when we're done."

Their feet scurried through the dirt path that led into the cabin and back to the Hudson Hornet. Benny opened the trunk once more and grabbed a few blankets, the same blankets he used to hide his rifle, handing them over to the miners.

"Here, take these. Looks like you'll need 'em. Keep yourselves dry and warm. It's a little chilly in that cabin of yours." Then he walked over to the driver's seat, with his men already in the car.

With Diego outside, too, he spoke in Spanish with happiness in his words.

"What the man say?" asked Benny.

"Thank you, gentlemen. You're all good men," Donato ex-

12

pressed, standing outside in the cold in his overalls.

"Oh, I don't know about that last part," Benny alleged, thinking little about his words. "Donato," he said.

"Yes, sir?" the poor man responded.

"Your English is pretty good! Where'd ya learn it?" he added, smiling from one side of his mouth.

Donato gazed at Benny's face. "I was born *here*, sir," he said.

"Right," Benny replied, before dispersing.

Chapter Three

To Each His Own

They were on the road for a few minutes now, following the instructions from the poor miners.

How many members were in the Comstock family? Could be anyone's guess.

But what they all knew was that the Comstocks were now marked by The Lost Dogs gang.

As instructed, Benny drove past Honeyspoon Farms, hitting forty-five miles-per-hour, then sped up the hill, just like Donato said, ensuring not to receive any attention from a third party, especially the Peacekeepers.

The Hudson Hornet was built for the harsh roads; softer suspension and tires built for dirt tracks allowed the car to dance along the road at high speeds, which was essential in Valport, where most of the mountain roads were dirty and uneven. Bright, glowing stars filled most of the night sky, along with the moon stalking the people of Knox.

More minutes had passed and eventually, the Comstock farmhouse was in sight; sitting toward the end of a large wheat farm. It had two floors, with the top holding a stunning balcony, which was wonderful for summer nights. There were light posts sitting along the white fences that surrounded the great wheat fields.

The path to the house was long with tall, drab oak trees that were equally spaced between both sides of the path, creating a beautiful shelter overhead with its leaves and branches. At the end of the path were two brick wall pillars, both supporting lights to illuminate the driveway into the Comstock family home.

Benny parked his car halfway through the path and switched off the engine, listening to the sound of crickets chirping.

"Let's go," he said, whilst removing the silver key from the ignition and opening his door, enduring the scent of manure.

He, like before, walked to the trunk, lifted it up and warily removed his precious rifle; carrying it like a briefcase. He closed the trunk and followed the lengthy path to the farmhouse. Houston and Desmond were standing to his left, Carson and Reese to his right. Although they were marching at the same speed, Benny was somewhat a few inches in front.

Approaching the house, he yelled, "Comstocks! We got some business we need to take care of!"

The tall, brown gate opened, as if they were expecting guests. But how could they have known?

"We knew someone would turn up some day, but what the hell is The Lost Dogs doin' on our farm?" questioned one of the guards from inside of the yard.

The men allowed Benny to speak for them—he was in charge, after all.

"So, you *do* know us? Which of you Comstock scum runs this place?" he spat at him.

"That sure in hell ain't any of your business. Get the fuck off our farm, you good-for-nothin' bastards!" wailed the other guard, standing by the side with his hand resting on a six-shooter revolver.

Benny noticed that his revolver was not all filled with rounds. Maybe two or three bullets, he noticed.

In the center of the yard was a large stone water fountain, but it was not in use. Flowers were growing on the sides of the house, as well as the sides of the gates and fences from which they entered. There were wheelbarrows carrying goods, a green horse wagon—but no horses—and a few cars, mainly pickups and sedans.

"That gold you stole, it don't belong to lowlifes such as yourselves," Benny explained. "Those miners work for *us*."

"We ain't askin' for you to—"

"Now, now, son. Let's see what this man has to say to us."

Swiftly, a round man, probably in his fifties or sixties, interrupted one of the guards and addressed Benny. He wore light brown pants, which were rolled up from the ankles, with a light blue and white checkered shirt, clean shaven and his white hair was cut very short.

"I am Comstock. Vincent Comstock. This is my son," he pointed to the young man he interrupted earlier, "Romero Comstock," he said, smirking from ear to ear.

"Well, thanks for the warm welcome, Mister Romero, Mister Vincent," Benny said, nodding his head at the two and returning a grin. "Charmin' man, ain't he?"

The gang sniggered.

"So, you said your gold belongs to *you*? You must be The Lost Dogs then, ain't that right?" Vincent asked.

"I see you're good with names, but stupid to know what the names mean," Benny acknowledged.

"What do you want? The gold? The moonshine?" Vincent asked, gazing at Benny and his men.

"Both, if you'd be so kind," Benny answered with a smile. "I ain't ever heard of anything about you Comstock folk. My guess is you came to steal what you could never build." Benny paused and glared around. "And what have you built? Nothin', by the looks of it."

Vincent's eyes jabbed toward Benny's face, cringing in response.

"This place ain't civilized. You steal the sweat of a man and pretend like it belongs to you," objected Benny.

Surprised, Vincent glanced at the intruders.

"You people aren't any different," he began, raising his voice and raising his chin.

"Are you willing to die for this gold?"

"We're all gonna die, Mister Comstock," expressed Benny, leaning in farther.

Benny raised his rifle, aiming the barrel first at Vincent, firing a round into his neck, then at Romero's chest, killing them both instantly. The Lost Dogs had opened fire on Comstock's men; prioritizing their aim at the guards that were closest to them.

Bullets flew like flies, tearing through the flesh of the thieves. Those who decided to fire back were shot before having the chance to aim. And those who were determined to run were shot, too.

"On the balcony!" shouted Houston, firing his Thompson.

Desmond supported him and shot at the upper floor.

More men appeared from the front door of the farmhouse and were shot by the gang. Blood poured down the front white wooden steps and onto the cobbled patio.

Before marching into the home, they reloaded. They hurried through the front door, pointing their barrels in front for any surprises.

"Come on out, now. If you value your miserable lives," announced Houston.

An older woman, about the same age as Vincent, had slipped onto the stairs, then tried running up.

"Hey!" screamed Reese, chasing after her.

A man had leaped out from one of the side rooms, the dining room perhaps, and into the wide hallway. The man was armed, but Carson quickly eliminated him before he could reach for his holstered pistol. Carson and Houston had now chased after Reese, who was pursuing the old crying lady.

"You're with me, Desmond," mentioned Benny, opening a door to his left.

Hiding behind some wooden furniture, a younger man had fired a shotgun round at Benny, missing him. Benny swiftly moved his head behind the door frame before he could take another shot.

"Boss, you holdin' up okay?" Desmond asked, troubled, as the empty shells smacked the wooden floor.

"Yeah, sure," replied Benny, taking cover behind a pillar. "Don't worry 'bout me!"

Reese, Houston and Carson were fighting more of the Comstock family on the top floor, but they had lost the lady.

"Show yourselves, cowards!" a man shouted over the gunfire.

"Ready?" asked Houston.

The three men had barged into the room and opened fire, killing whoever was present in there.

Desmond, too, had removed the man with the shotgun.

"You still got it in ya, son!" shouted Benny.

A light brown and blue paint were common across most of

the rooms' walls, along with white ceilings. Splashy paintings were placed on the walls, although they were not originals, and the carpets were white—now covered in blood and filth. Bullet holes scattered on the main floor's walls and doors, and spreading out on the stairs.

When Benny and Desmond had joined up with the rest, the house had fallen into sudden silence. But then they heard weeping from the master bedroom.

"You hear that, Boss?" mentioned Houston, staring at the door.

"Yeah, let's go," acclaimed Benny.

Carefully, they approached the white door to the master bedroom.

"These people *really* like the color blue," said Carson, giving a little chuckle.

They all stood behind Benny, who ran and kicked the heavy door with his foot, causing it to topple over and bang onto the floor.

All of a sudden, a man with a pistol aimed at Benny, but he was already determined to take him down, and so he did. Benny fired at his stomach. He did not die. Not yet, anyway.

A woman, the same old lady from not too long ago, had screamed. She was in tears. More like mourning.

"Well, what do you know? The old witch outran all of us!" Desmond said, laughing with the rest.

Benny grabbed the lady by the hair and held the white strands in his fist.

"Now, where is our gold, damn it?" questioned Carson, furiously.

"Fuck you! You killed my family, my sons!" she yelled.

The injured bloke that Benny had shot began crawling out of the room, until Reese shot him in the back once more, finishing him. The old lady screamed and ached simultaneously.

"No! No, no, no! My sons! You've killed them all! You bastards murdered my husband!"

"Unless you want to meet the same fate as them, I suggest you talk!" Desmond antagonized.

"In that safe in the bathroom," whilst pointing at the door, "and your moonshine is in the basement."

"That stuff ain't even worth savin'," Benny spoke softly in disgust.

Then he looked at Reese and flicked his head toward the bathroom door. Reese knew exactly what to do.

"Come on, Houston," Reese mentioned.

"You boys won't get away with this, you hear?" the hag blared.

"*Away*?" Carson began, "You won't be tellin' anyone. You ain't got nothin' no more."

"All of you, you're all going to die! You're all *evil* people! Your boys' luck will run out soon!" she continued to snivel.

"*Life* is an evil friend, ma'am," Benny suggested, leaning in closer to her, "and lucky people are those who are prepared to die. So, tell me... how lucky are you?"

Her annoying cries became louder without any pauses in her breath.

Heavily stomping, Houston and Reese returned from the bathroom with a few small fabric pouches.

"We've gotten the gold!" said Houston, loudly.

"This is all they had, Boss," Reese explained.

"Is that it?" Benny responded in shock.

"Well, it'll have to do," said Carson, walking away from the master bedroom.

Benny harshly removed his fist from the woman's hair, resulting in her to fall to her knees.

"That's all we took," she said, desperately, tears rolling down her wrinkly face.

"What're we doing with her, Boss?" asked Desmond.

"Let her be," Benny replied.

One after another, they left the bedroom, leaving the woman sobbing on the floor, and headed for the narrow wooden staircase. When pacing down to the first floor, ignoring the bodies and pools of blood, Benny stopped and thought of an idea.

Chapter Four

When the World's on Fire

Benny turned around, projecting his words to the rest. "Go into the basement, grab as much moonshine as you boys can carry, and meet me outside. Oh, and if you find anything valuable, take it."

He slowly walked to the front of the farmhouse, assessing the rooms at his sides. There was a large dining room to his left and a spacious living room to his right. It was a large family, after all, he thought, before proceeding to walk toward the pretty fountain.

The men had returned from the basement, prancing up the stairs, each carrying one jar of moonshine, and journeyed through the front door.

"That'll do nicely," Benny began. "Run into any trouble? Find anythin'... useful?"

"Only this, Mister Falcon," said Houston, bobbing his head at the jars they all carried.

"Oh, there ain't nothing but dust down there, Boss," acclaimed Desmond.

"I thought these weren't worth savin'," Carson mentioned, lifting the moonshine up to inspect it.

"We ain't savin' 'em. We're burnin' this whole place to the ground. Let them know it was an *accident*," replied Benny.

"Who?" asked Reese.

"Any witnesses, the law, the public, whatever," Benny said, quietly.

"I like your thinkin'!" shouted Reese.

"All right, grab a jar and just splash it all over the house, the fields and anythin' that we ain't takin'. Be sure to splash the bodies," Benny declared.

Looking at the Comstock house, he spoke, "I'll start with the house. You boys sprinkle it on the wheat fields. Just make sure you do enough sprinklin', fire'll spread quick, anyway."

As the gang began spreading the moonshine on the wheat, Benny walked back into the basement, grasping a jar of moonshine by the neck. "Nasty stuff," he whispered to himself.

He spilled moonshine as he hopped up the basement stairs and trailed it outside to the yard. There was just enough moonshine for the sticky trail to end at the driveway gates. The men, one by one, returned to the basement to grab more moonshine jars.

"That weren't enough?" Benny asked his men.

"They're tiny jars, brother," Reese responded.

"Should be done with one more," said Carson, walking toward the big house again.

Sometime later, the interior of the Comstock home was coated with the sticky moonshine and the trail lead outside, past the tall driveway gates and onto the long path. His men had finished sprinkling the booze onto the wheat farms—both sides of the path—and formed a trail of alcohol to merge with the alcohol Benny had poured.

"All done?" questioned Benny, trying to catch his breath.

"Yes, sir," said Houston.

The thick scent of dirt had evaporated from the air, now replaced with the scent of strong, dry moonshine; like walking into a paint factory.

Benny reached into his inner pockets, locating one of the

few cigars he always carries before pulling it out and licking the mouth piece a few times, then holding it between his teeth. Reaching into his trouser pocket, he revealed his engraved flip lighter.

He handed his gun to Houston. "Grab this a sec, son," he said, placing his free hand over the flame to ignite his cigar, then closing its lid. Houston returned Benny's rifle.

"I'm proud of you, boys. You didn't get shot this time," Benny started. "Couldn't have done it without you fellas."

"It's who we are, Boss," explained Desmond. "Well, who we *used* to be."

"Just a few cuts and scratches, but we'll live," said Carson.

Shortly after, Benny, who had only smoked about half of his cigar, tossed the remaining burning chunk onto the alcohol trail near him. The fire began spreading, following the path the men created; hurling toward the house and the through both sides of the wheat field.

Slowly, the wheat began to burn before spreading quickly, like a virus, torching the rest of the fields. And the wooden farmhouse house had shot up in flames almost immediately, creating an acrid smell as the flames grew larger.

"That'll keep us warm!" Benny shouted, laughing and rubbing his hands together.

The men laughed.

Suddenly, the alarming sound of screeching tires was heard arriving at the end of the long road.

Who could it be?

Chapter Five

The Dark Road Home

A small bullet flew past the men, and another penetrated the chilled dirt below them. They were stunned; hearts racing fast.

They did not expect another fight, as everyone on the farm and home were dead, except for the miserable hag, that is.

Rushing for cover through the thin, knee-high wheat, they hid behind the thickest trees, peeking out their heads to establish who the new threat was.

As the fire grew larger and stronger and its heat ripped through the fields, The Lost Dogs understood that it was time to leave—or perish with the chaos they had created.

"Keep your heads down!" Benny stormed.

"Ah, shit! What the hell is it now?" exclaimed Houston.

"How should I know?" responded Benny. "Just return fire!"

"Boss, they don't look like Peacekeepers!" Carson called out, moving his head down.

"Don't matter! Kill 'em all!" shouted Desmond, whilst feeding a magazine into his M50 Reising.

"Lucky for us, these bastards ain't good at shootin'!" said Reese, ducking behind the thick trunk of an oak tree.

Although Benny and his men were determined to eliminate the new threat, the amateurish band, whoever they were, made it easy for The Lost Dogs to take them down. Regardless, the men knew it was a force they had to eliminate.

It was night, approximately seven-thirty, and the only lights illuminating the farm now was the fire that was rapidly spreading and the lustrous moon above.

As the raging fire grew, the strangers, whose bodies were now kissing the dirt, wore denim overalls; some a light blue and others a light yellow, heavy leather boots and plain white t-shirts, and most of them were armed with a Colt 1911 pistol.

"They're lookin' like farm boys to me!" said Benny, firing at the last standing man in the left collarbone.

When the farm became silent again, they heard the crackling of the blaze, scorching the farmhouse and heating the backs of the men.

"Let's go see who they were. Just don't finish them off if they're still breathin'. Let them be. It ain't our problem no more," explained Benny, trampling through the field.

"Best be quick, Mister Falcon. Or your car'll burn, too," said Reese.

Looking down at the bodies, Benny squinted in awe. "They're just young men, damn it." He slowly turned around. "Let's go home."

"They had it comin' to 'em. What can you do?" muttered Houston, before holding his rifle by his side.

Before the flames had surged farther, The Lost Dogs had returned to the car. Quickly, Benny lifted the Hudson Hornet's trunk once more, placing his machine gun into the trunk.

He swiftly returned to the driver's seat and squatted in, placing his pistol onto the dashboard, a pistol he kept for emergencies. "Just in case," he said, peeking into the rear-view mirror and carefully reversing out onto the almost frozen main road.

As he drove away, the flames grew larger, ripping through the fields and igniting the Comstock home, like a sunrise burning a clear sky.

"Well, we all did a fine job! It's not every day we destroy an entire farm," Benny announced. "We'd better get home before your wives kill me."

"Or Valentine will probably kill us all if we're late to her dinner again," Houston mentioned, glaring at the fire in the rear-view mirror.

"Could've gone a lot smoother, to be honest," Reese added, nudging Desmond who was not interested.

"You don't say," Carson said, quietly.

"Hey, lighten up a bit," began Reese.

"You're both idiots," said Desmond.

"Funny," stated Houston.

The men began arguing and yelling, and Benny had clenched his teeth, chuckling at the rest. With the utmost caution, Benny made his way home sensibly. He did not want to draw any more attention—it was a long, strange night, after all.

As the men progressed toward the miners' cabin, the light from the flames began to diminish behind them.

"We gonna let Al know about what happened?" asked Houston.

"I'll explain it to 'em. We wreak of smoke and fire. He'll catch on, anyway," replied Benny, calmly.

"Whatever you say, Boss. Al ain't gonna care much," added Houston, who peaked out of the window.

"Those Comstocks weren't anything special," said Reese. "Not like it matters who we did it to."

"You know," Carson began, "he's right. We got the job done, didn't we? Still, it weren't what we expected."

Suddenly, the screaming sounds of sirens were heard rushing past the men on the other side of the dark, frosty road. It was a vibrant red fire truck, along with two deep black police cars, racing through the night and heading toward what was once a welcoming, pretty farmhouse.

"Best get home quick, before, well... you know what," said Desmond, turning his head around, watching the vehicles rush by.

"Do me a favor, boys. If your kids ask why we smell of smoke, just let 'em know we sat around a campfire. Your wives'll know what it means," said Benny, constantly eyeing the gloomy road ahead and his silver door mirror.

The men nodded and hummed in agreement.

"And if they don't understand, well, have fun explaining it to 'em!" Benny laughed.

The road ahead was somber, and Benny drove carefully. It was quiet. The streetlights skimmed into the car when they passed them, creating soft flashes.

Although they were silent, the men understood the thoughts of one another without a spill of a single word.

As Benny drove farther through the empty roads, the tall trees invited a peculiar memory; The Lost Dogs were approaching home soon. In this area of Valport, the trees were always towering on the hills and the roads were mostly murky. And as for the grass, it always seemed to have a light touch of green during the wintertime, as if the color was washing away. The thin, white clouds were dissolving into the sky, allowing the beautiful starlight to luster down on the town of Valport.

"Valport truly is astonishing at night, 'specially this time of year," Carson said, gently.

"Oh, yeah. That's one of the reasons why we stay here," Benny responded, scratching his cheek.

"Plus, we got more respect here than we do anywhere else," said Houston, staring out of the lightly steamed up passenger window.

Desmond chipped in. "This *is* home, after all. Only place we *really* belong to."

"Always have, probably always will," Reese added.

"Knox ain't half bad."

Benny paused before exhaling deeply.

"This place is... feral. But it's *home*. Sure, we're an island off the coast of Boston, but the state couldn't care any less for folk like us. So, it's easier to get work done out here. Anyway, we best get back to the shed, the shack, hut. The miners."

As the heavy car drove smoothly over the worn-out asphalt, Benny reached for the chrome radio knob, turning it gently clockwise. He smiled when the sound of violins and trumpets began to echo through the cabin, reminding them of home.

"Music feels better at night," Benny said, softly.

Gently, he tapped his fingers on the top of the steering wheel, synchronizing his knocks with the beat and distracting himself.

Above, the clouds created an overcast, covering the sky like a blanket and blocking out the beautiful moon and starlight.

Slowing down after missing the turn, Benny carefully reversed backward, placed the car into gear and then turned into the dirty side road, which lead to the cabin.

Light droplets of rain were pelting the windscreen. Even though the rain was fast, the droplets were very thin and almost invisible. It was only when they smashed against the ground that the raindrops became observable, as the tanned, dusty ground had become darker when swallowing the rain.

Swiftly, Benny parked the Hudson Hornet outside of the withered cabin, pointing the headlights onto the ill-lit path.

"You gentlemen stay right here. I'll just drop this off. Don't go wandering off now, you hear?" said Benny, opening the car's door.

As he planted his feet into the dirt, the cabin's filthy door had opened, causing Diego and Donato to parade out.

"Mister D and Mister D," shouted Benny, smiling and jaunting toward the two.

"What happened, Mister Falcon?" queried Donato.

"We got your gold back. And like I promised, they won't be threatening you fellas no more."

Benny put his hand out to Donato. "Here," he said, reaching into his inner pocket and revealing the small pouches. "The gold. That's all they had."

Surprised, Donato stared through Benny's glasses, and he understood that the man before him was serious. "Did you kill them?" he questioned.

"Kill 'em?" Benny returned the question. "How else do ya think we got the gold? What, we just asked for it and they handed it back?" he supposed.

"Jesus," Donato whispered, glancing at the ground. "Please, give the gold to Mister King, sir."

"You sure 'bout that?" Benny raised an eyebrow. "All right, I'll do that."

Benny dug the small pouches into his inner pocket.

With his hands together, Donato arched his back and said, "Thank you, amigo."

"You're safe, you hear? You and your friend. Stop worryin' so damn much," said Benny, stepping toward Donato. "And, what happened earlier... Al didn't tell us who we'd be meetin', so we didn't mean to startle ya," Benny proclaimed, placing his hand on Donato's shoulder. "We're headin' home and re-member, this *never* happened. Best keep your mouths shut!" he yelled after marching back to his Hudson Hornet.

Donato, with a last cry, shouted toward Benny, "You're good fellas! All of you!"

"No, we ain't, brother. We just did what was necessary," Benny alleged. "Goodnight," he continued, sitting comfortably in the driver's seat.

Slowly, he turned the silver ignition key with his right hand, steadily pulled the choke outwards next to the steering wheel and pressed a shiny button quickly, which caused the heavy engine to start and rumble.

With his right hand tightly gripping the leather steering wheel, he leaned partially to his left, peeking out through the window, into the door mirror and reversing his car back down the hill before turning it around.

"Odd folk livin' here," said Houston, whilst staring at the miners.

"That's normal for places like these," replied Desmond, rubbing his eyes.

Benny felt stiff and fatigued.

They had joined the main road again, heading home through the darkness to The Lost Dogs' manor.

Although they were *all* tired, Benny was frazzled, yawning constantly on the way home and wiping heavy tears from his eyes.

The law was already on their heels right about now, and with that in mind, they had to return home hotfoot.

Chapter Six

Our Solitude

As they returned to their den—The Lost Dogs' manor—Benny parked his car in the driveway, revving the engine as quietly as possible to not disturb the family.

"Home, sweet home," said Benny, grabbing his pistol from the dashboard and leaving the Hudson Hornet.

"It's good to be back," Houston mentioned, exiting the car.

Carson, who was the last to exit, since he perched in the middle, replied under his breath, "Tell me about it. 'Specially after tonight."

Reese was stretching his arms upon leaving, whilst Desmond had rubbed his palm on the side of his neck, slowly massaging it.

Suddenly, Missus King—Caroline King—left the manor and marshalled her husband into the yard. She was only a few years younger than her husband, Al, had her soft, dark brown hair in a bun and wore a long black dress.

"Oh, Jesus," Benny whispered.

"Where've you boys been?" she exclaimed, her hands resting on her waist.

"We sat around a campfire," responded Benny.

"Oh, don't talk smack to me, boy!" said Missus King, infuriated. "You're late for dinner and you smell like burnin' shit! Get yourselves washed and changed, and you best do it quick, or I'm tellin' your wives what ya'll been up to."

"Caroline, honey," Al stuttered, "give them a break. We'll talk about it later."

She swiftly looked at her husband and then glared viciously at the rest. Without saying another word, she exhaled and stormed off to the big manor.

The men laughed amongst themselves.

"Anyway," began Al, "how did it go?"

"You might be surprised," said Carson, chuckling.

"Go on."

"Our miners had problems. Some of our gold was stolen, Boss. You know *that* part of it. But we did manage to get it back," said Benny, reaching into his pocket and revealing the purple velvet pouches. "*However...*" Benny paused and then continued to look at Al directly, "we burned down the Comstock farm. The people that *stole* the gold."

"You did... *what*?" pressed Al, his face displaying confusion.

"Told ya you'd be surprised," added Reese.

"Boss, those fuckers ain't nobody. It don't really matter," Houston also added.

"And what makes of this Comstock family?" enquired Al.

"Dead. Killed 'em all first and then we took the gold," mentioned Carson. "We didn't have a choice, really."

There was silence between them, and Al felt more relieved than angry.

"We didn't get into any trouble, either. Just got the job done, like you wanted, Boss," Desmond suggested.

"The burnin' part was *my* idea, Al," Benny informed. "Best thing to do against people like those Comstock folk. Of course, we didn't want it to escalate, but it did. Unfortunately."

Before turning to the house, Al nodded and eyed his men, glancing at their stinking clothes.

"That's not what I hoped for, but at least the job got *done*.

That's what matters. But you still fucked up. Go on. Get changed, get clean. You don't want to be late for Valentine's dinner. We've got some talkin' to do."

When he finished, Mister King trudged along the path which his wife dragged him through and returned to the luxurious front doors.

"Let's go," said Benny, and herded the rest into the warm manor.

The front double doors were tall and wooden, and were painted in a deep brown coating, supported by a large brown doorframe with thin floral windows on each side.

The interior was vibrant, containing soothing colors that relaxed the eyes, like the white and cream flower carpet, a walnut double staircase in the main hall leading to the first floor with flowers carved into its handrails, red and gold vases resting on cabinets in the hallways, and silver and white chandeliers dangling from the ceilings throughout the manor, creating warm craters in the halls.

Most of the walls were plain white, and some were painted light brown on the bottom-half, supported by white on the top-half. The doors were polished walnut, too. There was a common theme with whites, browns and polished walnut furniture, aided by floral patterns; either carved in or stuck on.

It was lively with children running around, the television playing *Crusader Rabbit* and the wives of the men were preparing the dining table. But when Benny and the men had trod in, the women goggled at them in disbelief.

"I'll inform you ladies later," said Caroline, placing the white dinner plates onto the long wooden table.

"Uncle Benny!" yelled a young three-year-old girl and

grabbed Benny by the left hand.

"Hey, little princess," Benny replied, looking down at her tiny face.

"You smell," she added, then giggled.

"Oh, yeah? Your dad smells worse," he replied and chuckled. "Go play, sweetie," he said. "We'll join you shortly."

She assessed the television and then ran over to it, sitting down quickly to join the other children.

"Don't bring the smell in here!" scoffed Caroline. Benny and the men looked over at her and raised their eyebrows.

"They're going," mentioned Al. "Go upstairs, get clean and come on back down," he continued, as he waved with his hand, like telling a cat to shoo.

"Yes, sir. Yes, ma'am," responded Benny, smiling and acknowledging Caroline's annoyance.

He took to the long, white stairs and up to the second floor of the manor, where a soft, white carpet had blanketed the floor. Benny's room was at the end of the hallway; its brown walnut door stared at whoever had climbed the steps. He removed his black leather shoes and lifted them off the delicate carpet, carrying the pair into his welcoming room. Slowly, he reached for the polished chrome doorknob and gently pushed against it.

The carpet from the hallway continued into his bedroom, spreading from corner to corner. It was a large room, fitting for a couple—but Benny was not married. No, in fact, he was the only member of the gang who had never had a wife. A king-sized bed lay against the light brown and white striped wallpaper, a color combination and pattern that matched the carpet. Most of the furniture was crafted from walnut or oak, along with the curtains adorned in brown and white floral patterns, and two silver lamps on each side of his bed.

Of course, like everyone else, Benny had his personal touches; a short bottle of caramel whiskey with a small glass beside his wardrobe and a collection of his favorite vanilla cigars resting in a box on his desk. On his bedside table stood a frame—a portrait of a beautiful woman smiling at the viewer. Benny had always glanced at the photograph, for it was the photo that had kept him company in the lonely room for years. His croaky voice saddened as he lifted it from the desk.

"After all these years, what have I become, Ma?"

Chapter Seven

The Family Dinner

Excitedly screaming and rushing into his room were the children of the other men, jarring the door open.

"What're you doin', kids?" questioned Benny, tiresomely. "Let me get changed and I'll see you downstairs."

"But you have to play with us before dinner is ready," said a young girl, waist-high to the man.

"Yes, please!" yelled a boy, a lot shorter than the girl, parroting her behavior.

Before he had the chance to respond, more young children stormed into the room, thundering with shouts and screeches.

"Uncle Benny! You stink!" arrived a taller girl, maybe seven or eight years old, her black hair in a braid.

"Uncle!" and "Let's play!" howled two little, scruffy boys, both donning black jumpers.

At this rate, Benny was afraid of being late to dinner!

Benny took a deep breath and addressed the children. "All right, all right! Listen, kids. Let smelly Uncle Benny shower and I'll be downstairs in a few minutes. We'll have some fun, but you best get to bed early tonight. Oh, and don't get Missus King angry."

It was quiet when a young, dazzling woman had walked into the room. She was twenty-seven, slim and had pale skin along with dark, brown, warm hair.

"Come on, children, dinner is almost ready. Get to the dining room and stop annoying your uncle."

Her voice was soft and gentle, and the children had listened to her, proceeding into the hallway. She donned a white, silky dress, patterned with black spots.

"Thank you, Sloane," Benny said, calmly.

"I'll leave you to it, *Boss*," she smirked and her delicate eyes stared right into Benny's.

"Funny," he responded.

"What is?" said Sloane, smiling at the half-naked man.

"You callin' me *Boss*. Since when did Mister King's grand-daughter work for me?"

"Take me tomorrow," she chuckled.

"Ya know, sometimes you scare me more than your grand-mother," he laughed and waved his hand at Sloane.

"I'll see you downstairs, Mister Falcon. And don't be late, Benny. Please."

"I won't, so don't you worry," Benny confirmed.

Her dress had spun as she turned and walked out of the door, leaving the scent of peaches behind, and her footsteps were light; almost difficult to hear.

The warmth of the steam had covered him as he carefully left the shower and headed toward the wooden door, stepping into his brumal bedroom. Benny coughed and shivered, as if his bedroom was covered in ice and snow.

Slowly, he wore his silky, gray, stripey pajamas, which were wrapped up in a dark red, woolly bathrobe, and his feet were embedded into a pair of cushioned black slippers. He quickly wiped his thin spectacles and hurried downstairs, lest the ladies start yelling at him.

"Evenin', ladies," Benny called, addressing the women. "Gentlemen," he said, watching the other men.

"Come, take a seat, Son," implied Al, as he sat down on the

head chair.

"Valentine's been *real* busy this evening. She's cooked us somethin' special, so you boys best finish your meal," said Caroline, smiling as she placed a hunk of meatloaf into her dinner plate.

"She's always cookin' somethin' special for us. That's why we love her," said Benny.

"I'm flattered," replied the beautiful young woman, who was the same age as Sloane.

She sat on the couch, along with the children, who were distracted by the television.

"Start eating, or no television for tonight," said Sloane, as she, too, sat with Valentine.

The elegant ladies sounded like angels, and with that, the children obeyed them.

As per usual, the wives sat with their husbands, and Benny perched on the head chair opposite Mister King.

The dinner was exquisite; meatloaf made from ground beef, peas smothered in melted butter, fresh chopped vegetables, creamy mashed potatoes, thick gravy and crispy thin fries.

"Drinks, anyone?" asked Al, as he stood up, reaching for a tall bottle of red wine.

They all granted, placing their wine glasses toward the end of the table.

"Wine, Benny?" prest Caroline.

"No, thank you. I'll behave myself tonight," responded Benny.

"You... *behaving*?" replied Caroline, releasing a little laugh.

"Yes, ma'am. Tell you what, I fancy some Coca-Cola. Ice cold, if you don't mind," noted Benny.

"Are you serious, boy?" said Caroline, who seemed confused.

As the men gazed blankly at Benny, the ladies began to chipper.

"What?" Benny started, watching everyone in the room. "I have a bad taste in my mouth. *Not* from the food, obviously. From... *you know*," then stared directly at Al. "Hey, Caroline, you should take more rests, like your husband. Blow some steam out of your ears," Benny grinned.

"Quiet, Mister Falcon," she hurled back, feeling peeved.

"Give the man a Coca-Cola," said Al, looking at his food. "He might stay silent... for once."

Caroline passed him the thick glass bottle after releasing the cap.

"Wine ain't really my thing. And I ain't in the mood for any whiskey," Benny muttered, placing the chilled bottle to his lips.

"Rum?" asked Mister King.

"Don't," said Caroline, leaning over the long table to fetch more peas for herself.

"Beer?" Houston asked, looking at Benny, as he was swallowing the Coca-Cola.

"Forget about it," he groaned, returning the chilled bottle to the table.

"Vod-," Reese spoke, before he was cut off by Carson's sudden elbow nudge.

The family had concluded their meal. It was delicious, as the only remains were crumbs and gravy stains on the plates.

"Valentine, honey," Al alarmed, peering over his shoulder toward her, "That, my darling, was delightful! As always."

THOSE LUCKY FELLAS: PART 1

"I appreciate that, Mister King, thank you!" she responded, smiling with her rosy pink cheeks.

Caroline had cuddled with the children nearest to her, and they felt warm in her arms as the television continued lighting their eyes.

"And for dessert," Sloane announced, "I've made some of that chocolate cake everyone likes. I made two, so that's plenty to go around!"

"Oh, yes, please!" said Benny, as he sat up in his chair.

"You ladies outdid yourselves," mentioned Al, who began slicing through the delicate cake.

"Thought I'd help Valentine," she replied, placing a slice of her home-baked chocolate cake in front of Benny.

The scent of melted chocolate consumed the rooms.

Not too long after, the ladies had left the table and headed into the cozy living room, leaving the men behind.

"Fellas," Al King began, "We gotta talk. About... you know what," waving his hand slowly over the wide table.

"Yeah, we do," replied Benny.

Together, as the women returned and wiped the table, the men had moved into the snuggly sitting room on the opposite side of the long hallway.

The luminous moon was stalking the night sky, casting a vivid glow and ridding the darkness of Knox. It was calm, yet damp and chilly, as the brisk wind had breezed slowly past the tall pine trees.

There were very few critters; most could not survive the coldest February nights, but the larger animals found it somewhat acceptable, as the owls and foxes slept soundly, occasionally calling out in the night.

"I asked for you gentlemen to give a few threats. That should've worked," commenced Mister King, whilst sitting cozily in his brown armchair.

"It didn't work, Boss," mentioned Carson, who was leaning against a display case which contained old photographs of Sloane's childhood.

"Things got out of hand real fast, Al," stated Reese, who was immediately backed up by Desmond.

"They were stubborn bastards," he said, "and they weren't showing much respect. Ain't no way we could've talked out of it."

With his eyes moving from one man to another, Al stared at Benny.

"Discipline," added Houston, "is what we gave 'em."

"You killed the entire family *and* burned the goddamn house down," Al retorted. "That was far too much."

Benny was sitting in another armchair, brown and soft, like the one Al had dominated.

"You're awfully muted, Mister Falcon," Al mentioned.

"They've already said. It got outta hand. We needed to show discipline. You know how it goes," he replied with tiredness in his tone.

"The plan didn't go accordingly. Why'd ya burn down the entire farmhouse? That weren't necessary, don't you boys agree?" continued Al, as he eyed the room with his remaining eye.

"Plans change. They always do. We were sendin' a message. Think of it as leavin' a mark, without a trace, of course," Benny explained.

Al did not seem satisfied with their remarks, and it was not oblivious, as Al had pulled a frown.

"Look, Boss, I don't know what to tell ya. I'll be honest, it *was* a little out of character, but we did what needed to be done. We *always* have," Benny reassured.

Still thinking about the situation, Al impugned, "And what if they come after us? Here, in *our* home."

"They ain't comin', Al," responded Desmond, as he thumped his hand down onto his knee.

"If they do, we've never failed to give 'em a good fight. That's why we're still here, still breathin'," Carson implied.

"And it's why every gang in Knox hates us, every one of us folk," Houston voiced from across the small room. "Because they can't touch us."

"Let me tell ya, they don't like us because they can't get rid of us," said Reese, stepping forward toward Al.

"He's right," Benny reasoned, "and you know that better than all of us, Mister King. Peacekeepers may get involved, but heck, them other gangs won't. And *if* they do, you know how it ends."

Al nodded, slowly looking around at the men who were leaning against the furniture or sitting, then drawing his eyes at the floor. He was disappointed, but he had a reason to be.

"Fine," he aided himself. "But I expected better from you all. You're all meant to be havin' my back."

"Fair enough," gritted Benny, drowsily.

"We've *always* had your back, Boss," Desmond added.

As their conversation grew, the men felt dimmed, struck with boredom, and their eyes struggled to open. Benny, on the other hand, had both eyes closed, with Al's voice becoming muffled and slowly beginning to fade.

"Hey, Al," stated Benny, grabbing the attention toward himself. "You mind discussin' this some other time?" he asked, as he raised his eyebrows, forcing his eyes to open.

Al had become more aggravated. "All I'm sayin' is that you fellas are professionals. You've been doin' this shit for *years*. Me having to sit and talk with you ain't a *normal* discussion. It *ain't* right," said Al King, as he stood up from the comfortable chair.

"We're gettin' old, Boss. Thought we were putting this life behind us," responded Benny, smiling directly at the old figure. "This conversation is goin' nowhere. Just forget about it."

"Let's stop this, then, enough!" yelled Al, who was beginning to become frustrated, as he flicked his hand to where Benny sat. "It is late, so I'm headin' to bed. Goodnight, gentlemen," he bided, crunching his eyebrows and skulked out of the room.

Caroline, who had just heard her husband, entered the sitting room, glaring at the tired men. "Why does my husband seem agitated?" she asked calmly. "Benny?"

"You're *always* believing I've got somethin' to do with everythin'," he replied with a grin. "Never mind," the tired man added.

"Well, get some rest, boys," said Caroline, who turned around and was halfway through the doorway, "It's been a long day."

Wiping his face from his forehead to his chin, Benny had rested his head against the soft chair.

"Goodnight, Uncle Benny!" howled the children, as they galloped across the sitting room, like ponies up a hill.

"Shush, kids. It's far too late to be yelling," Sloane said, softly, who was following the children to their rooms.

Benny chuckled, "It's all right. Goodnight! And don't be

givin' Sloane a hard time," he said, turning toward the graceful woman, "G'night, Sloane."

"Goodnight, Benny," she countered with her angelic voice.

A few minutes had ticked by, and the ladies had left the dim-lit living room and called for their husbands to walk with them to their snug, tepid bedrooms.

"Oh, well," started Houston, who was already up when his wife called for him.

"You need a hand gettin' up, old man?" Carson sniggered.

Benny smirked at Carson, and he could see the other three men stretching in the corners of his eyes.

"That's funny," he said, rubbing his tired eyes using his slightly cold fingertips.

"Your bed is gonna stay cold if you don't get up," Desmond mentioned, reaching out his hand toward Benny.

"Time for bed, Boss," said Reese, who had his arms above his head, stretching them vertically.

"No, thank you. I'm sittin' here for a little longer. Got some... thinkin' to do," Benny acknowledged.

"'Bout what?" wondered Houston.

The men had stalled, like a deer in headlights, and stared at the old figure sitting in the chair.

"Don't stop me from thinkin' and don't keep your wives waitin'," retorted Benny.

Confusion struck the men, but they had their orders from their wives and their boss, whose mind was beginning to doze into the abyss. Carefully and silently, they left the room, leaving Benny to snooze, like a baby in a cradle.

Chapter Eight

Midnight Radio

The night grew colder, with frost bristling against the thin tree branches and coated the cars in a thin white sheet. There were no streetlights nearby, and it was only the moon that flared like a lightbulb.

And the house?

It had its perks.

Situated in isolation, it was quiet. It was peaceful. It was the way the men enjoyed it; almost hidden from the rest of Knox, where they could peacefully live with their wives and children, knowing they were all safe.

The sitting room, which was once warm and inviting, was now brisk with cold air travelling from wall to wall. A very dim light was lit against a cabinet, illuminating one side of the room. The cold had provoked Benny, waking him up from his nap.

"Jesus," he said, sitting up in the armchair and fastening his bathrobe.

He used his fingers to brush his hair backward and stood up, stretching his back first before his arms and legs simultaneously, then shivered.

"Damn, it's cold," he uttered to himself.

Gently, the withering man journeyed into the dark kitchen, flicking on a small lamp that illuminated a small portion of the room's corner. He placed his chilled hand on the knob of a wooden radio, turning it ever so slowly to receive a broadcast. It was playing America's national anthem, but Benny paid little attention, so long as there was noise to keep him company.

Yawning, Benny prudently hoisted the metallic lid to a silver cake container, revealing Sloane's delicious cake from earlier.

"Now we're talkin'," he whispered, placing a slice onto a white dinner plate.

The heavy fridge door was wide open, rattling the glass bottles inside and Benny peeked, mouth ajar.

"It's goddamn empty!" he cried.

Although the national anthem began to fade, Benny was alarmed by the noise approaching from the stairs, when suddenly, Mister King had routed downstairs.

"Hello, Benny," he said, squinting his eyes over to the man, who seemed a little startled.

"Boss," acknowledged Benny, who mutely closed the fridge door.

"What're you doin' awake at this hour, son?" Al posited.

"Same reason as you, I guess. Hungry or thirsty?" he asked.

Al picked up a glass beside the sink and let the tap run, then collected the cold water and raised his eyebrows at Benny.

"You, son?" he entailed.

"Both. But there ain't no milk. And we're runnin' low on orange juice," he said, moving his slice of cake toward himself.

Al swallowed his last gulp of water and turned toward the man, who began digging his spoon into the slice of delicate chocolate cake.

"Speaking of. I got a job for you tomorrow. It's a quick one, so don't worry."

"Let me guess. Grocery shoppin'?" he said, grouchily.

Al King smiled. "Spot on, my boy!"

Benny nibbled on the cake crumbs and replied, "First I burn down a house, now I'm doin' chores? So, whose money are we collectin'?"

Leaning against the chilly kitchen counter, Al beckoned, "The usual. Yours, mine and the rest of the money belongin' to the men. Oh, and the gold we took back, I'll need you to drop it off at my jeweler's store."

Benny licked the nippy fork and turned his head to face Al, who was already watching Benny closely, like a hawk.

"Ain't we supposed to be collectin' all of that at the end of this month?" he asked his boss.

"Well, we didn't collect last month's pay and the people already know we're comin'. I didn't want to startle people during Christmas time and early on in the year."

"Right. And what about this month's money?" Benny added.

"Leave it. We'll collect it at the end of the month," said Al.

"We could just get it all in one go, but you ain't willin' to listen," Benny said and sighed. "Fine, I'll go tomorrow."

"One more thing," Al continued. "Take Sloane with you. Let her do the shoppin'. She enjoys it too much."

Still shivering faintly, Benny noted, "And in the meantime, I'll do the collectin'. Got ya."

"Goodnight, and don't be up for too long, Benny," said Al, as he carefully treaded out of the kitchen, leaving the man in the ill-lit room.

As the old clock ticked, Benny had placed his dinner plate and spoon into the sink, allowing them to soak in warm water, and quietly paced up the grand staircase, heading into his lonesome bedroom.

THOSE LUCKY FELLAS: PART 1

It was toasty. At least this time. The old, gray man had shed himself from his cozy robe and slippers, and gently sprawled onto his bed, letting out a deep grunt after tucking in.

Intently, he removed his glasses and settled them onto the bedside table, parallel to the picture of his beautiful mother.

He tossed and turned until eventually managing to fall asleep before the room went cold.

Today was a strange day. But tomorrow? Even stranger.

Chapter Nine

A Dog with Two Tails

His sleep was irksome. The bitter cold was biting his skin through the night. He did not sleep very well. But the morning warmth of the house was welcoming and refreshing. It was ten minutes past ten.

Meekly, Benny rubbed his eyelids using his dry fingertips, yawning very widely. He sat up, dangled down his feet to feed them into his slippers and stood, carefully stretching his withering bones.

"Christ," he murmured when he heard his spine crackle.

With leaden steps, he shifted toward the window and slowly departed the curtains, then placed his worn fingers into the blinds and moved them up to peek outside. The sunlight was blinding, and he squinted before removing his fingers and repositioning the curtains again. There was a mellow knock on the door.

"Come in," Benny responded.

Sloane had been brought into the room by his words.

"Good morning," she said, soothingly.

"Mornin'," he responded, turning his head toward the lady.

"I wanted to ask what you would like for breakfast," she sought an answer, whilst swinging herself from the side of the thick brown door.

"Tell you what. I fancy somethin' a *little* heavy," he put forth. "Eggs and bacon, please. Oh, and two slices of toast. And throw in any of that meatloaf from yesterday, *if* we have any left," he aggregated.

"Sure," Sloane said, grinning from ear to ear.

"What?" Benny noticed her smile.

"Nothing," the glamorous woman reacted, still smiling and causing the old man to smile, too.

"I'm hungry, *starvin'*, to be honest," Benny played along. "Would you kindly pour in some orange juice, please? And a dash of whiskey with that, too."

"On it, *Boss*," Sloane disclosed, as she vacated from Benny's door.

Returning from the bathroom, his face was washed, and his teeth sparkled. Then, he oiled and combed his dark gray hair and friendly mutton chops, before slipping into a fresh, clean outfit, similar to that of last night. The man sprayed some cologne onto his buttoned shirt, tie and sleeves, and wore his spectacles after wiping them.

Carefully, he holstered his Colt M1911A1 pistol under his left arm, then headed straight out the door. Reese was standing at the end of the hallway when Benny closed the dense door behind him.

"Mornin', Benny," he said, observing the children through the wooden railing above the steps.

"Hey, Reese," he replied. "How's it goin'?"

"Just waiting for the wife to get ready," he added. "We're going fishin'. Carson's tagging along, bringin' his family, too. You want in?"

Looking out of the big window ahead, on the other side from where they both stood, Benny shook his head. "I got work to do, but thanks, though."

The bustling sunlight had filled the bright, white halls of the manor, creating a composed feeling for the members of The

Lost Dogs. A few nights of dreary rain had ceased, and the sun felt glorious.

"What sort of work you doin'? Collecting money?" Reese declared, cheerfully.

Benny returned a smirk. "Matter of fact, I am."

He looked at the old man, baffled. "Ah, right. Wait... Ain't we supposed to be doing that at the *end* of the month?"

"You know Al. He's never leavin' things as is. Always changin' plans."

"Yeah," replied Reese, releasing a sigh.

Without hurrying, he proceeded down the steps after patting Reese on his shoulder.

"Enjoy your fishin' trip, brother," said Benny, cheerfully.

"We will, Boss. Have fun with your trip, man."

Benny nodded, and Carson entered the main hall before stopping and watching him descend.

"Hello, Boss," Carson kicked off, "I was gon' ask. You wanna come fishin' with us?"

"No, I got work to attend to. Got a busy day ahead of me. But thanks, anyway," said Benny. "Where are the other two?" he proclaimed.

"Oh, Desmond and Houston?" Carson asked, itching his moustache.

"Yeah, them," Benny replied, closing his eyes when answering.

Reese, who was slowly making his way down the cream-colored stairs, included himself in the conversation. "Desmond's gone for a drive with the wife and kids."

"And Houston said the wife wanted a picnic with theirs. My guess is they're probably in the park," Carson input.

"Park? What *park*?" asked Benny.

"The park by the woods," Reese added.

"Right," said Benny, slowly, and adjusted his spectacles. "Well, you boys have fun. I'll see you in the evenin'."

"Why? You need somethin'?" asked Reese, who appeared perplexed.

"No," said Benny, breathing heavily out of his nose.

"We'll let 'em know you asked, anyway, Boss," mentioned Carson.

Both men nodded at Benny and began marching out of the tall, deep brown double-doors and into the open yard.

In less than no time, their children began to waddle out from behind them, with their mothers calling out. They stopped and smiled at Benny.

"Mornin', ladies," Benny acknowledged, as the ladies tilted their heads.

"Hey, Benny," said Reese's wife, softly.

"Have you had breakfast?" Carson's wife put forth.

"On the way," replied the gentleman.

"Well, hurry it up!" she replied. "Sloane's waiting for you."

"Yes, ma'ams," he said. "Enjoy yourselves and give those men a good smackin' if they misbehave."

The women giggled and said goodbye, then turned toward the front of the home, urging Benny to head for the kitchen and enjoy his breakfast in peace.

Stepping into the warm kitchen, which was heavily scented with the aroma of bacon and eggs, he watched Sloane prepare the golden breakfast.

"You've outdone yourself again, Sweetheart!" Benny exclaimed, looking over Sloane's shoulder and at the sizzling eggs.

"Thank you," the graceful woman endorsed, pouring the fried eggs into a dinner plate.

She tepidly picked up the greasy bacon strips and placed them beside the eggs, then sprinkled a little dash of salt and pepper on both. As for the meatloaf, she had returned it to the counter after spending a few minutes in the scorching oven, where it had joined the bacon and eggs.

"Benny, you don't mind your toast being *slightly* well-done, right?" she giggled.

"What've you done this time?" Benny said in response, pouring himself some fresh orange juice.

"I *may* have forgotten about the toast," Sloane said, still grinning at the man.

Benny, climbing onto the spongy seat of a barstool, watched his blackened toast approach the table.

"Oh, you've *definitely* outdone yourself," he said, goggling at the toast, which had its crust moderately blackened.

Cautiously, Sloane planted the breakfast in front of Benny, who was gazing at the still purple crocuses outside of the kitchen window. The brilliant sunlight had flourished on the island of Knox and despite the window facing away from the sun, it was still bright enough to cause a glow in the kitchen.

"Finally, we get some sunshine. Had enough of the damn rain," said Benny, who began to tear the toast and bacon strips, and place it into his mouth.

"It's nice driving in the rain," Sloane added, as she watched Benny rip the meatloaf and eggs with his fork, "but we could use a clear sky now and again."

Immediately as Benny finished his breakfast, Valentine had wandered into the glittering kitchen.

"Good morning," Valentine avowed.

"Morning, Valentine," Sloane returned, as both women smiled at one another. Meanwhile, Benny turned and tilted his head; eyes following her like a moth to a flame.

She approached the two and stood beside Sloane; both women dominating similar light blue woolly dresses, black leggings and black flat shoes. The scent of peaches had engulfed the kitchen.

"I've brought you your long coat, Benny," Valentine mentioned, smiling at him.

"Thank you, darling," he replied, sipping on the last drops of the delicious orange juice and whiskey mix. "Any chance you brought my cigars?"

"Of course," she announced. "And your lighter, too, or you'd go crazy."

Benny chuckled.

"Can we take Valentine with us?" Sloane asked calmly.

Looking at the two in wonder, Valentine was curious. "Where are you both headed?"

"Benny and I are going to fetch groceries," said Sloane, "and he's got some work to do."

"I can come," stated Valentine, "I don't have anything else to do this morning."

Both women looked toward Benny, who felt their gaze without a turn of his head.

"Sure, why not? The more the merrier," the old man alleged. "It's been a quiet day so far. I'm hopin' you two can make it lively."

Jolting the stool against the tiled floor, Benny stood up and reached for his dishes before Sloane and Valentine beat him to it.

"Right," Valentine began, "I'll wash up and you get ready."

"Go wait in the car, we'll be over in a few minutes," said Sloane, who was grabbing the creased shopping list from her pocket.

"That was in your pocket the entire time? You could've let me have a peek," Benny put forth, grumpily.

"*We're* doing the shopping," she replied, pointing at Valentine and at herself.

"Well, I ain't interested in readin' it anymore. You lost me," he mentioned, walking away from the kitchen and securing his long coat from a silver peg.

As the burdensome front door was plucked from its pretty frame, Benny had trudged toward his black Hudson Hornet; its slightly dirty metallic paint reflecting the sunlight into his glasses.

An unexpected, bony hand had grabbed Benny's stiff shoulder, causing him to freeze. He steadily turned around and saw Al present an eerie grin.

"Mornin', Benny!" he called out, still resting his hand on Benny's shoulder.

"Hey, Mister King," he responded, "What's up with all the yellin'?"

Al, potently, moved his hand onto Benny's back, then began speaking faintly into his ear.

"You're creepin' me out, Boss."

"Listen, son, follow me. I got somethin' I wanted to show ya. Keep quiet and stay close."

"What in God's name are ya doin', Al?" said Benny, as he was pushed to the side of the manor, feeling confused and disgruntled.

A short elderly man appeared to be seated on the backyard's dark brown varnished bench, peering into the undisturbed sea. He was garbed in a light tan Gambler hat, a green checkered shirt, brown pants and dark gray overalls, and his long white beard was a little filthy; brown around his mouth and chin.

Benny gawked, his mouth slightly open, before he rubbed his forehead, then sluggishly wiped his face. There was a long, painful silence.

"Goddammit," he mumbled.

"What?" riposted Al, seeming cheerful.

Turning his entire body toward Al, he looked in disbelief. "You gotta be kiddin' me, Al," he said, shaking his head.

"He's only here to visit, Mister Falcon. Nothin' else," said Al King, who began to depart, leaving Benny alone.

Kindlily, the strange old coot rose from the bench and walked toward Benny, who was staring back emptily.

"Benny, my boy!" he acclaimed, loudly, arms stretching out and ready to greet the man.

"If it ain't Otis McDonough. The hell you doin' back *here*?" Benny probed as he exhaled through his mouth.

Otis, squinting his eyes, glared back at the gentleman before him. "Is that how you meet an old friend, you ugly bastard?"

He wrapped his arms tightly around Benny, leaning into him, and Benny returned the gesture, except very lightly.

"*Friend*... is a... a bit of a stretch," said Benny tiredly.

"Come on over here," suggested Otis. "Let's have a chat. For old time's sake."

Stumbling, Otis marshalled Benny to the rather brumal bench. As they sat, they could not feel the cold as their thick winter clothing shielded them.

"I'm surprised you're still here, Benny," Otis voiced, directly. "Thought you might've left this place—this *life* behind."

Looking to his left at Otis, Benny reached into his long coat's inner pocket for his favorite vanilla cigar and engraved silver lighter. He offered one to Otis, but he declined.

"Why would I?" he attested, stowing the cigar into his mouth and setting it alight.

"You know... Get married and all?" continued Otis, watching Benny inhale the cigar's thick smoke. "Ever think about startin' somewhere new? I mean, you had it sweet on that lady. Eleanor Belle, was her name?"

The smoke blew gently, like a breeze against a dead, dry leaf.

"How'd you remember that?" pressed Benny, coughing lightly. "And besides, me and sweet Eleanor Belle. We..." he paused. "Well, we *did* want to settle, and she accepted me for who I was, but..." he paused again.

Otis leaned into the bench, resting his frail back onto the hard wood, and revealed a disappointed look. "Let me guess. Her parents refused?"

Benny huffed and cleared his throat.

"Quite the opposite," he said, burning more of his tasteful cigar and breathing out the heavy smoke. "*I* never saw a good man in *me* and a lady like her deserved better. So, as usual, people move on. Well, *she* did. I wrote to her and never got a reply. Wrote again, same story. But that was *years* ago."

Placing his wrinkled elbows onto his brittle knees, Otis

leaned forward this time, directing his words at Benny, as if he was spitting.

"So? Move on. Honestly, you're a fifty-eight-year-old mess, you know that?" bobbing his head whilst spitting his remarks.

"I don't know, man," started Benny, withdrawing the cigar from his dry mouth. "I never found myself another lady. This life, she's all I know. Ain't got nothin' besides these people, this home, and there ain't nothin' out there for me. That's *why* I'm stayin' *here*. Always will be. I stopped carin' about settlin' a *long* time ago."

Benny ploddingly tapped the cigar, settling the ashes onto the almost-frozen ground.

Otis frowned, "You still enjoyin' this work, you miserable fool?"

He held the cigar between his teeth, allowing the vanilla scent to roam his mouth. "She's all right, this life. I enjoy it, but I'm gettin' too old for this shit. You can't retire when you're wanted by everyone in Knox, right?" said Benny, lifting his head and closing his eyelids. The frosty breeze had brushed his face.

"Why not leave, my boy?" asked Otis. "I heard what happened last night with the farm. You've *really* let yourself go, boy," he added.

"You're *still* the idiot, aren't ya?" said Benny, who began to laugh in the poor man's face.

"Still jokin' around, Benny?" returned Otis.

With both his left index and middle fingers, he removed the half-burned cigar, clicked his tongue, and puffed out without hurry.

"Nothing in this world is gon' make me leave these men

and their families," he expressed. "And if I ain't leavin', then I'm staying to help. Even if it kills me. Besides..." he continued, taking another puff and filling his mouth with vanilla scent, "where would I run off to? And to be honest, we owe Al *everything*. The moment Mister King put a gun in my hand, my whole life changed."

There was stillness between the two.

"I'm retired," said Otis, traversing his head forward and then to Benny. "Oh, yeah! Eighty-one, finally retired, me and the wife. We startin' rentin' this old house from a nigger, a little cottage by the woods. Then we bought it. Moved in, decorated and all. It's a peaceful little place. Well earned, 'specially after spendin' a life on the run."

Ogling Otis, Benny leaned toward him. "Then why're you back here, McDonough?"

He returned a gaze. "I was comin' back to see the old gang. And, you know, I'm livin' a quiet life now."

Benny stared at the dirt by his feet. "You've always been livin' quietly, like a little fly in a field. Nobody really knew when you came and went—just like now. It's like you were... *invisible*!" he said, causing him to laugh hysterically.

"Enough!" Otis bawled. "Ain't no need for that!"

It was silent again before the charming singing of a white-throated sparrow was made clear.

"As useless as you were, you were good company," said Benny, eyeing the tiny sparrow. "I've missed moments like these."

Otis smiled and stared at Benny. "I didn't know our Benny was *sentimental*."

"I ain't," he said, reciprocating a wide grin, "I was kiddin'... about how I missed talkin' to you." Benny exchanged the thick smoke with fresh air, then breathed out slowly. "But I am being honest. You were useless."

A few seconds had rolled by, whilst the birds chirped, and the breeze had shaken the branches of the pine trees.

"I'm only stickin' around for a couple of days," Otis mentioned. "Don't go gettin' all emotional now."

Benny chortled, "Oh, yeah? Then what?"

Frowning, the old man looked at Benny through narrow eyes. "Then I'm headed back, ain't I? Dumbass," he answered.

Suddenly, there were unexpected guests arriving at the grand, black gate of The Lost Dogs' manor.

"Whoa," said Benny, quietly, as he steadily rose to his feet and leered at the visitors, adjusting his silver spectacles.

Who could this be?

Chapter Ten

I'll Be Seeing You

Cautiously, Benny headed toward the black gate, where Mister King was already present, and began staring at the two peculiar men with concern.

Above, the sky was still cloudless; rich sunlight radiating into the yard at the moment when Sloane and Valentine carefully opened the front door of the glorious manor and stood still, as if they were lifeless.

Benny, making his way toward his boss, turned toward the ladies. "Get back inside," he said, groaning.

His glistening silver chain of his pocket watch jingled as he trampled.

"Good morning, gentlemen!" the young man in the front piped, smirking from ear to ear at Benny and Al.

He bared a holstered pistol; a gray M1911 on the right side of his hip, like Benny's. The man with him, however, hogged a Remington Model 31 shotgun, with its barrel pointing at the dusty ground.

"Who the fuck are you?" Al challenged, irritated.

"My name is Vulpes," said the man in the front. "Vulpes Wonderwise. I'm a Peacekeeper."

They donned dark gray suits, along with plain, light blue vests and dark blue, silky ties.

And on their left lapel sat a gold pin, the emblem of the Peacekeepers; a human skull with no eye sockets and a rose in its mouth.

"I believe that ain't your real name," Benny sought.

Vulpes tilted his head and grinned. "Why not? You don't... *trust* us?"

"The law is using fake names, is that it?" questioned Al, lifting his chin.

"The hell do you people want?" Benny added, raising his voice toward the two.

Vulpes had glared at Benny and gently nodded, still grinning, "We got a *lot* of taking to do."

"No, we damn well don't," Benny scowled, stepping toward Vulpes.

"We heard about a *fire* at the Comstock Farm," continued Vulpes. "Just wanted to know if you gentleman saw anything... *unusual.*"

Al and Benny eyeballed one another.

"In addition to the fact that two young men walked up to our gate lookin' for trouble?" Al suggested, returning a smirk at the two. "No, we ain't seen much."

Quickly, Vulpes' grin was wiped from his face, and he brushed his hair back with his palm. "I see," he said, looking around before analyzing Benny's car. "That's a very nice car you got there! The *Hudson Hornet*. Never seen anything like it," Vulpes added. "How'd you get one all the way out here in Knox?"

Benny threw his cigar onto the floor, trampling onto its end. "Well, if you work hard—no, *smart* for once, you might be able to treat yourself, Mister Wonderwise," he said.

There was stillness for a few seconds.

"Turns out," Vulpes preceded, "there was one spotted at the Comstock's place."

Benny waited before thinking of an answer. "You sure? A

lot of cars look alike, don't ya think?"

"They *certainly* do, Mister Falcon," Vulpes replied, lightly nodding his head.

Leering, Benny squinted his eyes, peering over his glasses and suggested, "We ain't ever met before."

"No, we haven't," Vulpes answered, "but I know you're all dangerous folk. I'll give you the benefit of the doubt," the man continued, "I won't be foolish—not today. But you've been warned."

"Thank God you ain't as dumb as you look," Benny cited.

Vulpes snorted. "You fellas keep continuing this behavior and it might just get you killed."

"My men work for me, and *only* me," said Al, gesturing with his wilted right hand. "*I* decide when they die. And what *we* do, it ain't any of your damn business, Mister Wonderwise."

Closing his eyes and nodding his head again, Vulpes looked at the two men towering over him. "We just stopped by to ask if anyone's seen anything. That's all. No lawbreaking here, I assume," he voiced, smiling coyly.

Al tweaked his leather eyepatch. "Are we done?" he asked, looking directly into the young man's face with his one eye.

"Let's hope we don't meet again," Vulpes riposted.

"Here's hopin' we don't. Trust me," Al quelled and smiled, then raised his eyebrows, before leaning in farther. "Now, get the fuck outta my sight."

Both Vulpes and the other well-dressed Peacekeeper officer turned around and headed back to their polished navy-blue car. "Mister King," he said, adjusting his bowler hat, "Mister Falcon," he bid farewell, "it's a small world we live in. We'll see ourselves out."

THOSE LUCKY FELLAS: PART 1

He stopped in his tracks and turned to look at the two over his shoulder. "Remember, gentlemen, there's a difference between freedom and free will," Vulpes stated before they marched once more.

"Son of a bitch," whispered Benny, turning toward Al. "Now what? You think they *know*?"

"Now," he stalled, placing his thumbs behind his belt buckle, "we just play it cool. They're up to somethin'. Just need to be more cautious."

"Should we tell the others?" inquired Benny.

"No," Al swiftly responded. "Keep this between you and me. They ain't gotta know. Not yet, anyway."

Benny, bewildered, looked at Al. "Fine. Whatever you say."

When Benny turned, Al had nimbly gripped his arm. "If they try anythin' when you're out," he whispered, "kill 'em all."

"Yeah, I already know that," said Benny, gently removing his arm from Al's grip.

As he trekked toward his car and watched his boss stand by the yard's glorious gates over his shoulder, he called out, "Sloane! Valentine! Let's go have some fun!"

Otis had remained on the bench, frowning at the situation from afar. "What are you doin' messin' around with Peacekeepers, you dumbass?" he sulked.

"How did you know who they were?" Benny prest; his voice became a little lighter.

"I'm old," he remarked. "Their uniform has changed—looks like dog shit—but I know those bastards when I see 'em. Should've killed 'em when you had the chance."

Benny, heading toward his car, responded, "Not *here*. And *that* name. It don't sound right."

Hastily, Otis stood and shouted toward Benny, as Sloane and Valentine approached the car, too.

"Wait! Where're ya goin'?" he gave the third degree.

Both Sloane and Valentine smiled at the old man, opening the black car door.

"Shopping," said Sloane.

"Would you like to join us?" politely added Valentine.

"Sure," Otis decided, "and thank you!"

Benny, pointing his finger at Otis and holding the shiny metallic door handle, also expressed, "No, I don't want him yappin' in my ear."

"Why you gotta be so negative all the time?" exclaimed Otis, hopping snappily into the front passenger seat of the Hudson Hornet. The ladies giggled.

"Jesus," Benny stammered, entering the brisk interior alongside Otis, and the ladies nested in the back.

A pair of black leather gloves enveloped his hands, and he continuously clenched his fists to ensure they fit comfortably.

Soon, the Hudson Hornet was alive; its engine roaring in its bay and the pompous sound ringing through the hills and nearby towering pine trees. At a leisurely pace, the car accelerated toward the gates, where Al stood to one side, eyeballing the Hudson Hornet.

Benny paused by Al, lowering the window. "You need anythin' else?" he asked, causing Al to bend his back to level his head with the window.

"No, that's it from me," he replied, "but everythin' everyone needs is on *that* list." He pointed, then stood up straight. "Benny, you know *your* part."

"Mister King," he began, "we'll be back soon. Don't get

yourself into trouble, you hear?"

"Shut up, Benny," Al uttered.

The rather dirty car had rolled past the sturdy driveway gates, rolling through the dirt road which seemed muddy in the center from the rain last night, and onto the cold asphalt. The elegant ladies were perched in the back, gazing at the pine trees and the clear, charming sky; the sun radiating on their faces.

"Hey, Benny," said Sloane, leaning forward, "who were those men?"

He uttered after a short delay and continued to stare at the open road ahead, "Just some troublemakers, that's all. Don't worry about it. Nothin' to be afraid of."

The huge lake was calm; its water standing peacefully still as the blazing sun twinkled its light onto the surface, creating little stars. Birds jested and the residents of Valport were delightful, too! Women walked by dominating stylized dresses and skirts, and the men wore fine overcoats.

Little dust storms twirled against the car's wheels when driving through the pleasant country roads, and the vibrant strands of grass knelt against one another when the light wind swept through the fields.

The radio was faint, but the voice could be heard clearly; a woman reporting the news from last night, causing Benny to immediately switch it off.

"Car's still smellin' like fire, Benny," mumbled Otis, who had his crumpled hands rubbing together.

With his left hand resting on top of the leather steering wheel, Benny nudged Otis with his right, presenting a sulk at the man.

"What happened last night?" curiously asked Valentine.

"Nothin', honey, just some foul smell got into the car when we was out," Benny replied, quickly wiping the sulk from his face. "I'll get it cleared up once we're in town."

"I was wondering what that smell was," said Sloane, with her eyes searching the car.

"Anyway," suggested Benny, tweaking his circular spectacles to sit better on his ears, "we're here."

The whitewall tires rolled around a bend and Benny carefully parked the Hudson Hornet diagonally against a sidewalk, covering his car with a little shade, then cut the engine. People had rubbernecked the car, glaring at the fabulous machine from a distance. Even those that trekked by could not resist to stop, and stare. Otis reached for the shiny door handle until Benny jerked his shoulder.

"Hold on," he said.

"What is it with you now?" exclaimed Otis, as he turned around.

"Listen, we gotta visit Al's jeweler's store first. Got some money to collect, then you can do whatever you want," Benny voiced.

"Sure," said Valentine, exiting the car.

Sloane copied, and the rest followed. They had wandered onto the sidewalk, below the canopies of the local stores, and the ladies danced their eyes through the clear windows. Meanwhile, Otis was busy observing the roads and store signs.

"Damn," Otis said toward Benny, who was staring ahead, "*a lot* has changed since my last visit to Valport."

"And you haven't changed one bit, have ya?" Benny added, pacing up the sidewalk and pulling Otis from his bony shoulder.

The striking jewelry store was in sight; The Royal Shine, and they entered through the dark green, polished door.

"Lucky you, Sloane, all this is gon' be yours one day," said Benny, smirking at the pretty lady, who had also returned a smile.

"Good morning, ladies and gentlemen," said a sharp voice from over the glass counter.

The store was divine; white marbled floor, dark green painted walls, and a white ceiling, along with the bright sunlight seeping through the alpine windows.

"Mornin', Mister Sterling!" cheered Benny, roving over to the counter.

"Sloane and Valentine, too!" added Sterling, then rolled his eyes over to Otis, stunned. "My God, I haven't seen you in years, Mister McDonough!"

"Sterling, my boy!" replied Otis, who hugged the man over the glass counter.

"Honestly, how you missed this man is beyond me," said Benny, laughing at Otis, who began to frown.

"Anyhow, I've gotta run. Got some work that needs doin'," Benny said, plainly. "Oh, I almost forgot," said Benny, reaching into his pocket and removing two velvet pouches. "Here you go, Sterling! It's the gold Al wanted me to deliver."

Carefully, he nested the pouches onto his palm.

"Splendid!" cried Mister Sterling, "Thank you, Mister Falcon."

Mister Sterling wore a stripy pink shirt, topped with a dark green apron, like the color of the store.

"Mister Falcon," he said, nodding his slick, oiled hair, "Mister King wanted his earnings. I'll hand them over to you." He hurried toward the back of the store, then galloped back, handing over a white envelope. "It's all in there, sir."

"Thank you, Sterling," Benny replied, before handing the chunky envelope to Sloane.

"Here, hold on to this," he said, as she grabbed the bundle.

"You ladies want anythin' from here, just let Mister Sterling know," Benny suggested.

"We're fine for now," said Valentine, as both women headed for the door.

"Thanks, again, Mister Sterling," Benny stated, shaking the jeweler's hand and stepping outside.

"Hey, stay a little longer, why don't you?" Sterling asked, lifting his head over the clean glass counter.

Otis was still inside the store when Benny noticed there was no annoying coot by his side.

"We've got some work to be doin'. McDonough, you comin'?" he shouted.

"You go on ahead," he responded. "I've got some catchin' up to do with Sterling. Oh, and there's a car wash around the corner. The niggers over there'll give it a clean."

Benny rubbed his eyes from under his glasses and looked up. "Thank God. Give him a good thrashing if he starts gettin' all funny, Mister Sterling."

His laugh belled from inside the store, as Otis yelled back at Benny, who was too busy to understand the old man.

"Ladies," he said, turning to the two, "one more stop by my business, then you can go on your little trip. I'll fetch you somethin' to eat. You want ice cream?"

"Yes, that would be nice, thank you," Sloane replied cheerfully.

"Please and thank you, Mister Falcon," Valentine noted.

"Anythin' you ladies want," said Benny, who began to march toward his café.

"You're always spoiling us, Mister Falcon," said Sloane merrily, strolling alongside Valentine; both of their snazzy dresses rocking in the wind.

"I gotta take care of you both," he said, "or else Caroline would probably hang me."

Although the morning was cloudless, the wind was still nippy, and the air was thin and bitter.

Benny shivered and cocooned his neck with the tall, woolly collar of his long coat. "It's cool, but at least it ain't rainin' no more."

The gentleman and the ladies had crossed the quiet road, stepping onto the lightly frosted sidewalk on the other end. There it was, pervading on the corner of the street—Sweet Charm—an exquisite dessert parlor and café decorated in various shades of pink. Its pillars so polished they reflected the road they sat beside and replicated the brilliant sky.

"Hello, beautiful," said Benny, glaring at the store's shiny sign.

Sloane and Valentine sauntered behind Benny.

"You know, this store is older than the two of you," he said, grasping the tawny door's handle. "Should be open," he whispered.

Flamingo pink was layered onto the walls and the leather on the seats and stools was smothered in bubble gum pink. And the floor was most definitely covered in black and white checkered tiles, like a chessboard. There was no café in Knox that had seen a different floor.

The interior was very hospitable; framed pictures of Bing Crosby and Frank Sinatra hung on the walls, along with large street signs and flags of different states, accompanied by a great banner of the Massachusetts flag behind the counter, of course.

"Good mornin', Cassidy!" cheered Benny loudly.

"Jeez, Mister Falcon," replied the middle-aged lady in a pink overall dress. "You'll be giving me a heart attack some-day!"

As the party journeyed in, Benny glanced around the room. "Seems quiet today," he said, sitting on the colorful bar stool.

"Well," Cassidy responded, "it is early mornin'. It always gets busier during the day."

Cassidy altered her white hat and clocked her eyes at Valentine and Sloane. "Ladies?" she staggered, leaning over the white counter, "Oh, my goodness! You've grown up so much!"

The dazzling ladies climbed onto the stools beside Benny, who was cloaking his pistol with his dark woolly coat.

"Such a shame Benny doesn't bring you here often," Cassidy affirmed. "You're both *so* pretty!"

"*Thank you!*" replied the ladies.

The flashy rainbows of a jukebox brightened the corner of the café, drawing Benny's attention toward it, as he steadily sprung up and steered to its glare.

Cassidy eyeballed the old man and then expressed her smile toward the two women. "Anyway, what would you ladies like to eat?" she asked politely.

"Hook 'em up with some desserts, Cass, please," said Benny, poking the sparkly buttons of the jukebox until a mellow jazz began to play.

THOSE LUCKY FELLAS: PART 1

"Would you lovely ladies like to try our *new* special?" graciously asked the happy waitress. "It's two golden toasted waffles, one scoop of chocolate and one scoop of vanilla ice cream, and a dash of chocolate and maple syrup," she added, tapping her pink fingernails onto the counter.

Sloane and Valentine gently nodded with a smile. "*Yes, please*!" they requested together.

"Comin' right up, girls! Better get those sweet teeth ready," Cassidy responded, twirling around toward Benny, who began to approach his warm stool again.

"And what about the gentleman?" Cassidy queried, tapping her white painted nails onto the counter.

"Tell you what, Cass," the old man began to declare, "how about hittin' us up with three of your delicious chocolate milkshakes?"

"Yes, sir," she returned. "Now, I hope ya'll made enough room in your tummies! I'll be right back."

In a flash, Cassidy bolted toward the kitchen, leaving her customers at their stools. The sweet smell of sticky syrup and chocolate emerged from the kitchen's door, making its way over the counter.

As the two beautiful ladies spoke murmuringly, Benny fiddled with a newspaper and surveyed the front; just some gibberish, as usual, he thought. He folded the thick newspaper and settled it at the end of the counter before removing his leather gloves. Slowly, Benny placed his tired elbows onto the tabletop and interlocked his fingers.

Before long, Cassidy pushed through the kitchen's pale door, ambulating toward the counter, carrying two crowded, colorful plates and three freezing tall glasses of chocolate milkshakes, then placed them onto the table in front of her customers.

"Eat up, sweeties!" she said delightedly, placing the scrumptious desserts in front of the two ladies, along with their sticky drinks.

Prudently, Cassidy planted another in front of the grouch.

"*Thank you!*" said the ladies cheerily.

"Thank you, Cass," said Benny, sparkling his teeth.

"Enjoy it, folks! Holler at me if ya'll need anythin'. Don't be shy," Cassidy disclosed respectfully, turning toward the kitchen.

The whipped cream dribbled down the side of the congested, ice-cold glass, whilst Benny washed its straw through the chocolate mixture. He slurped up the flavorsome, thick milkshake, allowing the contents to freeze his tongue.

All the while, the women had begun to poke and tear at the hot waffles, breaking through the scoops of ice cream first, and indulged it in the gooey syrup. Subtle jazz music was still frolicking through the café; Cassidy began to whistle quietly to herself in the kitchen, as she cleaned the little spillage she caused earlier.

"How's your snack?" asked Benny, licking the corner of his moustache.

"It's delicious!" answered Sloane, placing down her shiny fork.

Valentine gently settled her milkshake. "It's really good!"

Benny smiled and nodded wilily. "Make sure you compliment Cassidy. It'll keep the hag happy."

The pretty ladies continued to nibble on their remarkable desserts; relishing each moment than the last.

It was serene. Then Cassidy wormed into the room, wiping

her skinny hands into a towel, and eyed her customers savor her work.

"Ya'll were either hungry or can't get enough!" she said, chuckling from behind the counter.

"This stuff is pretty great," noted Benny, settling the empty glass cup onto the table. "I should drop by more often."

Cassidy turned to Benny and rested on the counter opposite him before elevating both of her thin eyebrows. "Why don't you drop by more, you fool?"

Benny twittered and tried to catch his breath. "I've been busy. You know that."

Frowning, Cassidy lifted his empty, clouded glass and stationed it by the white pass-through window.

"So," she sighed, "why did you come by today?"

Benny did not move his head, but his eyes drove toward the woman.

"Money."

"Oh," the woman fretted. "Thought you'd at least give me a call first."

He raised his hand, silencing the waitress. "*Not ours*," he groaned. "I ain't in need of it yet."

The iciness of the milkshake rattled his throat, stimulating a harsh cough.

"Jeez, Benny," said Cassidy, placing her hand onto her chest, "you had me worried there."

"You keep startlin' yourself like that and you might never see your retirement," he laughed, and he was the only one who seemed amused.

Cassidy sighed and placed her palm onto her scraggy hip, then leaned her body to one side.

"D'ya hear about that farm that got burned down? Last night it was," she said, as her weary eyes stirred around the motley room. "They found some bodies in the fields. Some pretty *bad* stuff is going on in Knox."

Gradually, Benny's smirk melted into a thin, straight line. "I've heard about it," he said, shutting his eyes and tilting his head toward the ground.

She placed her towel into her skirt's small pocket and stretched her arms.

"Poor people," she continued, "but whose business is it to say?"

"Anyhow, speakin' of business," the old man declared, "How's it goin'? Anyone causin' trouble?"

Cassidy, who arose from the counter, straightened to face the grumpy man. "No, sir. Nothin' troubling here. But the café itself has been pretty busy!" she noted a coy grin.

Without haste, Benny nodded and picked himself up from the pink stool, stepping onto the checkered floor and pulled onto his coat's warm collar which hugged his neck.

"Good!" he affirmed, looking directly at her. "Be sure to call me if things get... *out of hand*. Thank you, Cassidy."

Pivoting toward the other two younger ladies, he voiced clearly, "I'll meet you both at the car in about an hour," before marching toward the shiny, reflective door.

"You're already leaving?" cried Cassidy, tightening her eyebrows.

Once catching the door's spotless handles, Benny peeked over his left shoulder. "I've got *business* to take care of, Cass. I'll see you in a few days. I'll bring the girls, too. They'll keep ya company." Eyeing the women, he stated, "And stay outta trouble, girls," then unlatched the door and stepped out into the bitterness.

With a stretch of his worn shoulders, Benny stood in the chill, peering at the noble sun. Although the clouds had ceased, creating a benevolent blue sky, the frost was blinding, and it was quickly erased by the cars which drove by; some classy, others glamorous and a few vivid, all crunching the frost beneath them, like stepping over dead, dry leaves.

Suddenly, Benny felt a hand forcefully tug on his arm.

Chapter Eleven

If I Were a Rich Man

"What're ya doin' here, Houston?" said Benny, feeling eased. "Ain't you supposed to be at a picnic?"

Houston tapped his fingers onto Benny's arm. "I ain't sleepin' in the park," he chuckled, before revealing a swollen envelope with green bills erupting from within.

"Damn," whispered Benny, glaring at the white brick-like object. "What in God's name have you been sellin'?"

Their heels began to march along the dull sidewalk, clicking fleetly, while Benny inspected his silver pocket watch. Seventeen minutes until noon, it read.

"Plenty of time," he mentioned to Houston, who was occupied with burying his envelope into his coat's deep pocket.

"Hey, Boss, you don't mind me taggin' along? After all, I am here."

"'Course not," said the older man. "I was gettin' our money for us all, but—"

"Your pockets aren't big enough," interrupted Houston. "That's why I dropped by."

"So, what *have* you done?" Benny enquired, watching him shrug his shoulders.

"Just... collected my own cash. Al said you was in town, so I thought I'd lend a hand. It gets a little boring in the house."

They continued pacing down the path, crossed the idle road and Benny undid the lock on the Hudson Hornet. The gentlemen sat in the car's arctic interior.

"Good Lord! You *have* to get her cleaned, man!" Houston

called out, sniffing and rubbing the tip of his nose.

"Yeah, I know. That's where we're goin' now," mentioned Benny, igniting the beast.

The engine prowled when he reversed onto the road, then roared as he cruised along the silent street.

There. A hand car wash situated between two buildings, both about three stories high—apartments, probably. No more than three colored men were waiting for their next customer.

Unhurriedly, Benny neared the car wash, springing over the curb and halting before lowering his window. The fresh scent of hot soap burst through in parallel with the aroma of wet concrete. At least it smelled better than the fire, he pondered.

"Mornin', amigo!" stated Benny, throwing a wave out of his window.

"Good morning, sir. How can I help?" replied the dark-skinned man.

"I'm in need to get this girl clean," said Benny, leaning more toward the chap, "but I'll need somethin' for the inside."

"You got a bad smell in there, sir?" he said, laughing.

"*Bad* don't even begin to cut it, my friend," Benny responded, opening the mucky door.

He passed over the keys. "Once you're done, just park it on the side somewhere and I'll be back shortly," mentioned Benny. "And *please*, get rid of that damn smell!"

"Of course, mister! You leave it to me," said the man, pleasantly.

Without delay, Houston accompanied Benny, and they both convoyed across the road, heading under the glacial shade.

"How's your business goin', Mister Falcon?" asked Houston, avoiding the cracks in the sidewalk.

"Pretty good, actually," said Benny. "Seems like your bar is keepin' well."

"Oh, yeah, The Wild Bull has really been stacked up with customers recently." Houston mentioned. "I was plannin' on bringing everyone to the bar after closing time. Ya know, like a family night out. But we gotta keep low... For now," he muttered.

"*For now*," Benny said, silently.

They paced down the slippery path, brushing through the people of the small town, and bid farewell to the buildings' shadows, like leaving a darkened cave.

"Wait," said Houston, reaching his right arm out to snatch Benny, catching him by surprise.

Otis, the bothersome old fella, approached the two, but he was quite a distant away to hear Houston.

"Fuck off," he mumbled.

"Yeah, about that..." Benny tittered.

"McDonough?" Houston asked, frustrated and facing Benny.

"Hey, it was a shock to me, too! I was more surprised the old-timer ain't dead yet," he replied, as Otis' short body drew close.

His sickled, wrinkled mouth loosened. "My God, Mister Alfrey! You've changed, but *still* ugly as ever," he said, clutching the poor man, forcing a hug in return, but Houston refused.

"That's funny coming from a caveman," he responded, causing Benny to laugh aloud.

"Not you, too," Otis added.

"Why don't you go assist the ladies?" Benny questioned, rotating Otis and poking his back.

"Fine, I will," he wailed, "At least they, uh... *respect me*... you sack of shits," he wailed some more, as his eyebrows draped and he stomped away.

"Anyway," Houston took control, "Desmond's butcher store next?"

"Lead the way, brother," said Benny, although he was already ahead.

It was a jovial day.

Their pockets were becoming stuffed with money, after all. As they approached Desmond's butcher store, The Country Sausage, a small queue was present inside; standing and enduring the stench of raw, bloody flesh. Nobody likes waiting, he wondered, standing erect by the store's thin, smeared window; juicy cow ribs and large sausages staring back at him, waiting to be taken home.

A quick whistle had struck Benny's ear; turning his head into a nearby alley and revealing a plump butcher. He was clenching another white envelope, too.

"I recognize th-th-that face," said the heavy man, stretching out his tubby hand.

"You work for Desmond?" questioned Benny, preparing to take the relatively thick envelope.

The butcher was cruddy, like he had lingered in a pigpen. "I d-d-do indeed. He t-t-told me you was c-c-comin'," he spewed. "I r-r-recognize that f-f-face."

"And here I am," said Benny, putting his hand forward, allowing the butcher to plummet the stack onto it.

"G-g-good day, sirs," said the fat man warmly, and turned down the tight alley.

"Very odd man," murmured Houston, as both men stared,

then wheeled round onto the sidewalk, coursing to their next stop.

Slender white clouds began to manifest overhead, but the sky remained radiant. They crossed the road again, turned left and walked steadily along the cold path, where an elderly man was poking his digits into the tiny buttons of a payphone.

"Easy, there, mister," said Houston, leaning against the telephone booth.

"Oh," replied the short old man, "seems like that was my last dime," he laughed.

"You all right, mister?" Benny grinned on one side.

The old man, who was too frail to return the telephone into its socket, looked at the two men and handed it over. "Here you are, gentlemen. I'm sorry."

Benny, grabbing the sage green telephone, arched his eyebrows. "Now, now, friend, what're ya apologizin' for?"

"Listen," added Houston, who reached into his pocket and revealed a leather wallet, "Take these. It's all I got," he said, handing over two dimes.

"Oh, no, don't—"

"I ain't askin'," said Houston, plainly.

His crinkled, pale hand opened, causing Houston to drop the dimes into his palm.

"Thank you, dearly. You're both kind gentlemen."

"You are more than welcome, sir," said Benny, twitching his head. "You need somethin', just ask, mister."

Whilst backing away from the misty telephone booth, they all bobbed their heads, and Benny and Houston rambled onto the rimy sidewalk.

Eventually, they had approached a garage—Deluxe Motor

Garage—its chalk-white sign stationed above its two blue, glossy, painted doors with one exposing a 1948 Tucker 48, drawing their eyes to its charming metallic blue finish.

"Jesus, Carson never told me he had one of these!" exclaimed Benny.

"It pro'ly ain't even his, Boss," Houston indicated, noticing him draw closer to the car veiled in the garage's thick walls.

Entering, Benny inspected its three chrome headlights, catching the sapphire blue sky and was amazed by its abnormality.

"Hello, there, mister," said the mechanic in a jumpsuit. "Can I help you?"

The unusual car was so polished it was as if they were all gazing into a mirror. Even the whitewalls were so clean!

"The name's Benny," he started, "I'm here on behalf of Carson."

"I see," said the soft-spoken mechanic. "He did say somethin' by that name was comin'. You fellas wait right here. I ain't gon' be too long," he said, pacing into a covert office around the back.

Shortly, he returned, carrying two swollen envelopes, handing them over to Benny.

"Jesus," Benny mumbled.

"Maybe it's our turn to open up a garage," whispered Houston.

"That's all he's asked to give ya," said the polite mechanic.

Benny nodded daintily before thanking him, then eyeballed the odd car. "Who does this car belong to?"

The mechanic, dropping his stained handkerchief into a toolbox, raised himself, ogling the men and the machine.

"Some young man dropped it off last night, askin' for a good ol' polish."

"Carson never told me he had one of these here," said Benny, squinting into his reflection.

"He never does," Houston stuck in. "It's not that impressive, Boss. Let's go."

"When do you ever see somethin' like *that*?" Benny asked excitedly.

With a friendly handshake, both men cleared off; the scent of engine oil deceased as they stepped into daylight. Like before, they continued roaming the chirpy streets of the small town of Valport.

"Gotta do one more stop for Reese," said Benny, stroking his friendly mutton chops, "then we'll head home."

"Let's enjoy the day, you know," responded Houston. "Take our time and *enjoy* it. And I *don't* wanna be seein' Otis."

"Fair enough," replied Benny, whilst trekking to their next store.

Beyond Buttons, it was called, the only tailor store in the small town. As a result, it was usually quite busy; clothing repairs, alterations and even any new fabrics would sell out fast!

"Reese should've come with you," said Houston.

"Why?"

"You know he don't stop talkin' sometimes. He woulda been good company," Houston tapped him on the shoulder.

They stood outside of the tailor store, staring at the magnificent suits on display.

"Too bad he loves fishin' more than his store," said Benny, opening the dark green and yellow door.

Without a doubt, the inside was gloomy, and it ponged of

fabric, of course. There were lumps of colored cloths, colossal rolls of patterned fabric and exclusive items of clothing on display by the luminous window and behind the mahogany counter. A pale ceiling fan was suspended above the counter, too, but it was immobile; they would be crazy to switch it on in this weather. Like most clothes stores, it was noiseless.

"Hello, gentleman," said a friendly thin face from the corner of the shadowy store.

"Mornin', friend," Benny replied. "I'm here for payment. Reese... sent me."

"Oh, sure!" the polite chap added. "Take a seat, please. I won't be too long."

"Thank you, kindly," added Houston, whilst Benny nodded in agreement.

"Gentlemen," the tailor said in a high pitch, "would you care for some tea or coffee?"

Both men looked at one another.

"No, but thank you," said Benny.

"You mind speedin' things up?" Houston declared, tilting his head toward the tailor.

Devoid of words, the scrawny tailor shifted into a shrouded room.

"'You all right, buddy?" Benny whispered to Houston, whose eyes were engaged with the unique clothing patterns on display.

"He's wastin' our time," Houston grumbled, deeply. "I don't like the smell of tailors. Nobody does."

"Cheer up, man. He was being polite."

The tailor returned momentarily, carrying a white envelope, just like before. He carried himself over to the men in dandy, dark suits; his footsteps muted on the carpet and delivered the half-full envelope.

"Here you are, sir," he said, avoiding eye contact with Houston. "That's all I have for Mister Reese."

"That ain't too bad, thanks. I'll give it to 'em, friend," Benny said, happily, then patted Houston on his stiffened shoulder.

"Thank you for dropping by, gentlemen," said the tailor nervously.

"I'll be seein' you around… probably," Houston said, as he stared at the tailor, like a hawk.

"Quit scarin' the man and let's go!" Benny grunted in his ear before dragging him out of the drab store.

The thin clouds began to thicken, polluting what was once a rich blue sky. Runty birds flew away from the clouds, searching for more heat to engulf their feathers in.

"Cheer up, Mister Alfrey," said Benny, patiently, compressing the envelope into his coat's wide pocket.

He pried his coat's soft lapels and reworked his collar, as he was already en route to his car; the marvelous Hudson Hornet.

"I'll go swing by and get my car," said Benny, travelling across the cheerful small town. Houston nodded, grunted and began stomping alongside the older, gray man once they had approached the harsh shadows of the buildings. But there was something odd about the car wash.

Without hesitation, Benny launched himself forward at the sight of a curious young chap inspecting his much-loved car.

Something did not seem right. *Something* felt… strange.

Chapter Twelve

Uninvited Guests

"Hey!" howled Benny; his eyebrows so scrunched they were stabbing his spectacles. "What in God's name are you doin', kid?"

Grabbing furiously onto his crusty plain shirt, Benny lifted the pint-sized young man to see eye-to-eye; his glare was enough to frighten the poor boy. He seemed to be in his early teenage years by the looks of his blemished skin and slim build.

"I'm sorry, mister," said the whimpering coward. "I was just *looking*!"

The dark-toned man, who had just finished polishing Benny's car, needled, "You, again? Ain't I warned you enough times?"

Benny eased off his shirt, allowing the boy to breathe. "*Again?*" he grilled.

Heavy breathing was heard from the coward, like a steam train chugging smoke, and he would not dare to run.

"It's that little shit," said the man from the car wash. "Always causin' trouble all over town. You work for that lady. What was her name?" he prest, resting his hand on his round hip.

"I can't say," mumbled the weakling, gazing at the ground in defeat.

"What *lady*? What're ya folks doin'?" probed Benny, towering over him like a tree.

The key to the Hudson Hornet was passed to Benny, acknowledging him and his fine work.

"Thank you, kindly. Here..." Benny suggested, "Keep the change, sir," and handed him a few extra coins.

"I appreciate that, my good man," replied the smiling chap.

It was as though Houston was invisible, standing by the scene. But he slipped in some words. He always does. "Listen, kid. This lady. What's her name? What's your business here?"

"She'll kill me if I—"

Without warning, the worm slipped, running into the distance, causing Benny and Houston to run, too.

"Get back here, bastard!" announced Houston, whose feet were so fast, he glided along the sidewalk.

"Keep goin' after him!" thundered Benny, lagging behind them.

Whoever he was, he dashed, and he was *fast,* ignoring the heavy garbage cans and the people that hugged the sidewalks. But, with luck in hand, he fell, and he fell *hard.* They watched as they heard a pair of bony legs scrape the concrete.

"I knew that'd happen," Houston said, catching onto his breath.

"Jeez," mumbled Benny, who was gasping for air, too. Together, they grabbed him, lifting him to his feet. "Now, take us to this woman," hissed Benny.

"You best not try anythin' like that again, kid. D'ya understand me?" warned Houston, opening his coat to unveil the pistol he holstered under his arm.

"All right, fine," agreed the filthy boy. "This woman... She's called... *Nora,*" he revealed, rubbing his bleeding knee. "That's what we call her. Nobody knows her *real* name."

"Who's *we*?" asked Benny, poking the man's shoulder, forcing him to turn around.

"Us people. You know? That know her—work for her," he supposed, secretively.

"Take us to this *Nora*," Houston said, sharply.

Without delay, the group meandered on the sidewalk, journeying into the quieter side of Valport, where most residents avoided, and for good.

"If I take you, she'll kill me and probably both of you, too! She's a stubborn woman," cried the slovenly man.

"Whatever she'll do to you, we can do a lot worse. Trust me," Benny added. "Now, shut your mouth and start walkin'."

Sprightly paint that had once splattered on the storefronts were now fading into nothingness. Windows were chipped and weeds sprouted from cracks in the ground.

As it turned out, they were escorted to Nora; they approached a small, grisly church that was rotting away on its own hill with its white wooden walls flaking and the roof tiles decaying. Like hedges, they stood at the foot of the broken-up path.

"I asked you to take us to that damn woman!" called Benny.

"She's in there!" bleated the sook, shocked by the old man's tone. "I'm being honest, mister. You have my word."

The chain-link fence wore a layer of rust and some of its wires were missing, creating larger voids.

"So... Nora's in *there*? Looks decommissioned to me," Benny questioned, eyeballing the church.

"Yes, sir. Nobody uses that church anymore, so we moved in," said the little bruised man.

"I didn't catch ya name, kid," said Benny, looking down at him.

"The name's Luther," he replied. "And your name, mister?"

Benny's eyes shot toward Luther, and he began strolling up to the dirty church. "It don't matter what my name is."

Neighboring the church lay a collection of old garden tools and a damaged wheelbarrow lay buried in the tall, uncut, dead grass. A lifeless tree suffered outside of its entrance.

Benny tried to remember when he last visited a church. But he could not recall.

Its double scabby doors were pushed in, creaking altogether as the company entered its cold, frowsy hallway; inhaling the dry, thick smell of concrete.

"Welcome to our kingdom, sirs," Luther chuckled, as he held the bulky door for the two.

Just as they entered, they noticed the white blotchy paint break into small rivers on the wall and the carpet felt muggy, but there were no holes in the ceiling.

"God, this is disgusting," Houston mumbled to himself.

Along the great, collapsed organ at the other side of the hall rested a group of youthful, besmirched individuals; about the same age and size as Luther, with some a few years younger, and they gawked at the strange visitors.

"You can't be bringing strangers in," barked a narrow, innocent voice.

"Nora won't like this," belled another.

"It's all right," Luther shouted through a cone he created with his hands.

"Where is she, anyway?" Benny grunted.

"She'll be here."

With heavy steps, Benny approached the juveniles, who settled around a makeshift table. He tiptoed, observing them like a wolf, and scanned their playing cards and the thin deck in the center. Lingeringly, Benny lifted his heavy hands, as if to calm the flock.

"What're ya kids playin'?" he pried timidly.

The young'uns peered at one another.

"Blackjack," said a soft voice.

"Ah, *Blackjack*. The most *fun* card game, wouldn't you kids agree?" Benny added, smirking at the lot. "Of course, I used to play it myself, but I ain't got much time for that sorta stuff."

His heavy heels danced against the stiff wooden floorboards when he circled the group. "Please, do carry on. I wanna see who... *wins*."

Thin, circular stones varying in different sizes lay on the wide tabletop, behaving like casino chips, accompanied by creased and crooked playing cards and cups of water—hoping it *was* water, that is.

Quickly, a child had slammed his fists onto the table and shouted, "Crap! I was winning." He seemed young, but too young to be a teenager.

"You gotta learn to give up and take a fall every once in a while. It'll do you great. Trust me," said Benny, as the child glared at him, disgruntled.

Houston roosted on a chair and raised his index finger. The card dealer, who was only a child supporting a shirt too large for himself, flicked a card in his direction.

With boredom, Benny stroked his facial hair and roved between the stained pews, finally resting against its harsh wood. Lazily, he reached into his waistcoat's pocket and dug out a cigar; a vanilla-flavored cigar and placed it between his teeth. He offered one to Houston, too, who politely declined.

"Mister," sprung out a voice from the table, "you can't

smoke in the house of God."

Benny looked over the dreary pew. "God don't care about us folk no more," he said and looked over at the immense cross hanging on the tarnished wall.

"You're not a man of God, mister?" questioned the same little voice.

"I grew out of it," said Benny, calmly. "I lost hope, and *it* lost me."

He rose to his heels and wandered once more.

"What about heaven? Do you want to go to heaven, mister?" the voiced echoed again.

"*Nobody* goes to heaven," said Benny, firmly.

"Damn it!" clamored Houston, as he watched his makeshift chips be swept away, then scanned a boy next to him. "You ain't cheatin', are ya, buddy?"

"No, sir," the boy sniveled.

Exhaling a heavy chunk of smoke, Benny revolved to Luther.

"Kid, you're wastin' our damn time!" he declared, picking the cigar from his mouth.

"I don't want any trouble, mister," Luther pled, sitting up at the sound of Benny's growling voice. "She'll be here, *I promise.*"

"You've already gotten yourself into a heap of trouble," said Houston, sharply. "And your ass ain't talkin' your way outta this one."

"We'll give it a few more minutes," said Benny, soundly.

"Then what?" echoed a voice from the narrow hallway. A lady—a pretty and young lady—stormed into the grand hall. "We don't get visitors around these parts, especially *your* kind. What are *you* people doing here?" she hissed.

THOSE LUCKY FELLAS: PART 1

"Afternoon," Benny stated, grinning from ear to ear. "You must be Nora. Lady with an attitude. Are you their godmother? What are you, like, twelve?"

Benny stepped slowly toward the lady and stood high, like a mountain.

"I am, and I'm twenty," she said, crossing her eyebrows beneath her dusty flat cap, "and I *know* who you people are. We have no business with folk from *The Lost Dogs*."

Smoke escaped from Benny's grin. "Quite an impressive lady you are, ma'am! But, oh, I think you do."

Luther's eyes widened.

"How so?" Nora replied, before resting her petite hands on her hips.

"Your boy, Luther," Benny pointed, "he needs to learn to mind his own business. That's all I'm here for."

In a flash, Nora rushed over to Luther and struck his face. "You should know better!" she snarled. "Lucky for you, you're still alive!"

There was an awkward silence. Luther had fallen from his chair and returned without spilling a word. Nora glimpsed at Houston.

"Who are you people, anyway?" he asked the angry woman.

"We're just poor people tryna get by. That's all. I'm sorry. We're *not* thieves. Luther doesn't know any better. None of them do."

"Well, there's that," said Benny, tapping the ashes from his cigar into an empty cup. "I thought we was tryna break into my car, but I was more worried as to why that little shit ran."

"I am sorry, sir," Nora blushed, feeling embarrassed.

"Tough world we got, ain't it?" Houston added, straightening his face.

"It's best if you men leave," she disclosed. "I know your type. There's no room for people like you here." Nora crossed her arms and took a seat on a firm pew; shaking her leg uncontrollably.

Tiredly, Benny stepped down the aisle. "Take care, ma'am," he uttered. "And don't make her angry again, kids," he added, as Houston joined him.

Again, Nora stood up and seemed worried.

"Listen," she called out, "Knox is changing. Gangs are no longer welcome here. And rumors have it, The Lost Dogs are on *that* list. And so are the Peacekeepers. No one wants those sons of bitches here, even if they are the law."

Coldly, Benny stared at the troubled woman. "Looks like you don't know much about us. We don't die so easily. Why do *you* even care, anyway?"

There was a silent stare from Nora. "You people *can* change. This island *is* changing."

Benny grunted and whipped his arm toward her, then proceeded down the aisle, stepping over the damp carpet, again.

"May God bless you folk," a meager voice dejected from a corner.

"I appreciate you not hurting us. After all, we know what you're capable of," Nora proffered.

Like a statue, Benny paused. "You people ain't as dumb as you appear to be."

Seconds slipped by and the men had trampled down the scraggy aisle and through the putrid hallway.

"We waited for *that*?" Houston asked by his side, grumpily, then drew open the stubby doors.

"I don't wanna be dealin' with more women," Benny replied. "It don't feel right, 'specially *that* type. Reminds me of Caroline."

"Fair enough," he remarked.

They drifted along the horrible path, feeling a pleasant relief when breathing in the cold air. The sky became pearly with thickened clouds; a canvas with various shades of gray. It was apparent that Knox will take another shower soon.

They had passed through the rusty chain-link fence once more, parading back to the more joyful side of Valport. Large crows flew into the trees to avoid the incoming bitter rain, but, with luck, there was a delay before the wet pellets plunged.

Before long, Houston opined, "So, are we keeping this between us?"

Benny, flicking the cap of his cigar onto the parky sidewalk, looked at him. "May as well keep it quiet. No need to bring this to anyone's attention. Ain't worth the effort."

They watched over the street and soon the ladies had joined them, lugging brown paper bags in their arms. And at the heels of Sloane and Valentine was Otis, tottering toward them. With his knuckle, Benny tapped Houston on the chest.

"Take Otis home. I'll take the girls."

Houston was not happy. "Ya can't be serious, Mister Falcon," he expressed.

"You have got your car, right?" Benny bounced back.

With his head sunk low, Houston swayed to his car; a black 1949 Cadillac Series 62, parked near Benny's. Its chrome bumper was so refulgent it matched the cloudy, peppery sky.

"Got your car cleaned, Benny?" asked Sloane, depositing

the bags into the Hudson Hornet's wide trunk.

"Sure did!" he happily cheered. "I had to once Otis had sat in it."

"What was that?" Otis yawped.

"Nothin', old man. Your ears are pro'ly playin' up. Houston is *kindly* takin' you home. Best behave now."

Otis veered toward Houston, who was waiting for the old coot to sit in. He detected his irritation when Houston snapped his fingers and pointed at him.

"Are we going with you, Mister Falcon?" Valentine asked politely.

Benny nodded, dumping more brown bags shopping bags into the trunk, before opening the door to let the ladies in. The trunk was shut carefully, of course.

Then, torpidly, Benny settled down behind the steering wheel, sparked the engine and rolled its whitewalls onto the main road, heading back into the steep, breath-taking hills.

"Should've sat in the front, ladies," Benny said ardently, relaxing his elbow on the door. "I look like a damn chauffeur."

Feeble giggles sprung from behind. With the cushiony suspension and monstrous engine, the Hudson Hornet frolicked over the hills, like a raging bull brushing through a field. Fallen leaves had soared into spirals by the edge of the road, then slept on the asphalt when the machine blew past.

"Slow down, Mister Falcon," said Sloane, surprisingly, as she wormed into her seat.

Valentine seemed agitated, too, as she wriggled into the cushy seat, calling out to Benny, "What's the hurry?"

He laughed and stretched his shoulders. "We're just havin' some *fun*. My girl's gotta purr now and again, don't she? And I ain't even goin' that fast!"

It was as if a layer of dust had draped the sky, preventing the sun's flaxen light from shimmering through, and instead, thin, barely visible, needle-like droplets plunged. The windscreen wipers swept ponderously.

Benny had driven over a small bump, and it was not long before a police officer emerged onto the damp road; garbed in a dark navy-blue suit and holding out his palm. Tardily, the car had come to a rest.

"Evening, sir," the cheerful officer chippered, marching over to the window.

"It *was*," replied Benny, and stuck his elbow over the door. "Why the sudden stop, friend?"

He hunched over and turned his head toward the road, pointing forward. "You see over there?" he said politely. "That tree's fallen over. No way around that, not until we clear it."

Benny held his head high, peering over the leather steering wheel. "A tree?" he caterwauled. "That ain't a *tree*, that's a damn *twig!*" he added, stabbing his finger in the air toward the fallen black cherry tree.

"I'm sorry, sir, but I can't let you go ahead," the officer returned with his hands behind his back.

"This world's gone *mad*," Benny mumbled weakly.

"Where are you people headed?" he queried.

Benny thought to himself, tapping his fingers lightly onto his lap and adjusting his spectacles. "We *were* headin' west. Up the hills. Guess I'll just take the other route," he drawled some more and slid his elbow off the door, latching onto the wheel once more.

The officer, pointing behind this time, offered some help to the miserable old man. "Sir, if you turn—"

"Yeah, I know the way," Benny's gnarl interrupted, "Thank you."

Just as Hudson Hornet turned, the respectful officer nodded his crown and waved. Naturally, Benny waved, too, but it was more of a flick than a wave. The passenger window had risen, and the narrow water pellets smeared the glass, flowing downward, like a river.

They travelled over the dewy road, noticing the sun dying behind a curtain of gray clouds.

Sloane's warm hand weighed on Benny's shoulder. "Everything all right, Benny?" her soft voice echoed. "You seem a little put off. Something wrong?"

His glowing eyes crept back toward her pale face. "It's nothin'," he grumbled, sighing immediately after. "It's been a strange day."

"How so?" questioned Valentine, leaning in toward the man.

Drawing himself forward, he coughed and tilted his head over to the ladies, but his eyes were fixed to the abysmal, glum road ahead.

"Anyway, ladies, how'd the shoppin' go? Find anythin'... *interestin'*?"

The ladies were snug, leaning their backs against the warm, plush, black seat, like they were sinking into a pillow of feathers.

"Usual shopping, you know. Food, ingredients and *lots of* popcorn," said Sloane gently.

"What sort of ingredients?" asked Benny, staidly.

Valentine leaned forward toward the gentleman. "I have a

new recipe you'll like, but I won't say. It's a surprise."

"What're ya plannin' on watchin' with *all that* popcorn?" Benny enquired.

"The kids wanted to watch Treasure Island. Thought we could all join in," said Sloane, smirking.

"It'll be fun, Mister Falcon," insisted Valentine. "Stop being so depressed."

A short, almost silent chuckle emerged from Benny; being repressed by the puddles of water slapping the tires and the rain pattering on the roof. Valport was a spec in the distance, disappearing altogether as the tall oak trees flashed over the horizon; their branches and twigs billowing through the raindrops.

As the sparkly radio knob rotated, static filled the time of quietude before a faint voice became audible—for the ladies, at least. Benny took no notice. Nonetheless, it helped him focus on the road and ease his mind; a distraction from this strange day.

Stopping by a bright red stop sign, he turned left onto a stringier road fringed by stone walls on either side and roved under a leafless grove of trees, making the exhaust quaver. The roads were almost deathly quiet, with the occasional pickup truck or family car sweeping by; usually red or blue. It was no surprise since most people avoided the thinner roads, especially during a terrible weather.

At short intervals, Benny tapped his fingertip onto one of the steering wheel's chrome spokes and slackly ran his fingers through his graying hair. His legs were full of lead, and it was because of the Hudson Hornet stomping over the ungainly road, making weighty thuds.

At last, they had arrived back at their home; their fortress.

The manor's cream-colored stone had darkened from the rain and had crafted puddles, as if it was weeping.

"Jeez, it's rainin' more up here!" said Benny aloud. "Wait 'til I park her up, then we'll grab the bags from the trunk."

Desmond stood by the black iron gate and waited for Benny to enter before securing it. The Hudson Hornet pulled up by the path and the engine was cut just after Houston departed from his onyx Cadillac.

Not long after, Benny, Sloane and Valentine dug themselves out from the car's warm interior, snagged the brown paper bags from the trunk and ran along the stone path leading into the serene manor. The thick, tall double doors were held open for Houston as he entered the snug hallway and shivered once inside.

"Thanks," he said, wiping his heels onto a rough, patchy floor matt.

"Seems like you beat us here," Benny said, wiping his feet onto the matt, too.

"I rushed over before the weather got a little upset," said Houston, catching his breath.

"I presume you saw the tree on the road," Benny supposed. "They closed it off, *that* road by the hill."

Houston stood up, staring with confusion at the man. "What tree?"

There was a silent stare from Benny. "Never mind," he declared, shaking his head and vacating from the door.

"Give those bags to me, boy," Caroline expressed, politely, throwing her arms forward.

She had drawn herself into the kitchen once Al presented himself.

THOSE LUCKY FELLAS: PART 1

"Gentlemen," he said grumpily, "we gotta talk. It's bad, *but* it's nothin' to worry about."

"Oh, this can't be good," mumbled Houston, as Desmond appeared from the brawny front doors, bobbing his head at the rest.

"We'll need to sit down for this one," Desmond supposed. "It's gon' be a *long* talk."

In an instant, Desmond's heart stiffened at the sight of a particularly stumpy fella.

"Well, if it ain't Desmond Kane!" Otis sung out, who had converged toward him in a flash and swathed his wrinkly arms around his torso.

The displeasure in his chest had riled him as he separated himself.

"You can't be serious," Desmond yammered, walking away from the pensioner and wagging his head. "Of all the people I know, *you're* the one to bounce back?"

Otis' steps expired and his angular arms lifted. "I don't understand why you crackers ain't even happy to see an old friend. The fuck is wrong with you all?"

His eyes feasted over the rest, and he walked into the cheery living room.

Strolling through the hallway, Benny laid his hand on Al's stiffened shoulder, encouraging him to walk by his side.

"So, where are the other two?" Benny asked, curiously.

"They're waitin' for us upstairs," replied Al, removing Benny's hand from his shoulder.

"Come. Follow me," said Desmond, turning around and leading the pack to the white steps.

Respectfully, Benny was a few steps behind Al, observing

the skittish old man twitch his bony fingers, and when they had reached the second set of stairs, leading to the second floor, Al's feet were in disarray. One entire foot covered the step and the other with just his toes and sometimes hitting or scraping the edge of a step.

They entered an ample sitting lounge, the first room to the right of the second floor; off limits to the children, of course. Like the rest of the manor, it was tinged in browns and whites, and floral patterns, too. Delicate white curtains with brown leaves splattered on its velvet were drawn by the long window, a white carpet accommodated by a cream-colored floral composition spread across the empty floor and a lengthy walnut table stretched from one side of the small room to the other.

"Boss, you all right?" asked Reese, opening the door and letting the men in. "You don't seem like yourself."

They all plopped down onto the polished walnut chairs, whilst Benny walked around the table, delivering their envelopes.

"Here you go, gentlemen," he announced. "That's all I collected."

Benny removed his long coat and flumped over at the table with the rest, meanwhile Carson poured golden whiskey into short square glasses and dished them out to the tired men.

"Right," Al began, standing over the table, "this little meeting we're havin'... It's about a *job*."

The men ogled their boss.

"For whom?" asked Carson, gently placing the whiskey bottle and joining them at the table.

The room was motionless.

Al strode to the wide window, feasting his eyes at the foliage. "Do any of you remember Mister Galvani?" he appealed, crossing his hands behind his back and grasping the whiskey glass with his wrinkly fingers.

"Lloyd Galvani?" asked Houston.

"Yeah," said Desmond, sitting up in the tough walnut chair.

Leaning in his chair, Carson put forth toward Desmond. "How'd you know?"

"Al already told me," he replied.

"That ain't right, brother," mentioned Reese, resting his elbows on the table. "You're supposed to share with us all."

Shaking his head after gulping down the drink, Desmond answered, "We are now, aren't we?"

Benny closed his eyes and sniffed the whiskey; burned wood, he noted.

"That's not the point," Carson included, swiftly.

"Listen," Al objected, taking a deep breath and turning toward the group. "Now, I know we ain't doing this... *work* no more. But we do owe him a favor."

Houston rubbed his face. "And what favor would that be?"

The room was calm, but only for a few seconds.

"He's got a job for us. We'll be robbin' a train."

Chapter Thirteen

We Were Young Once

"Oh, there's a relief," said Benny. His eyes widened, and he wiped his oily forehead with his palm. "I was gettin' bored of retirement."

Al planted his whiskey glass onto the table, glaring at Benny. "Keep your sarcasm out of this, Mister Falcon."

"*That* ain't a good plan, Mister King. What're ya thinkin'?" Carson trilled with his chin resting on his knuckles.

Reese probed toward Desmond, who laid back leisurely. "And what did *you* suggest?"

"Mister King only mentioned the job, that's about it," he replied. "I didn't think much at first, in all honesty."

Houston, who had already emptied his glass, poured in more of the smoky-flavored whiskey. "You should've just told us all at once. Like... *now*. In a meeting."

Firmly, Al clenched both hands and stowed them onto the table, taking a seat in the head chair. "I told Desmond first because he's got the biggest brain amongst all of you. And I wanted a second say in all of this."

Houston pointed his hand at Al. "We're *all* the second say in this, Boss."

Rearranging his glasses, Benny hunched over, poking through the air. "So... Mister Galvani asked us—*you* to do a job, and you *agreed*?"

"I ain't agreed yet," Al retorted briskly. "A few words were exchanged. That's about it. No agreements. No promises."

Minutes had passed, as they howled like wolves. It was

silent, then the hurricane of shouting and yelling came forth, then returned to calmness once more. Their eyes witnessed Al's crabbed face gaze at the table and then at the ring on his finger.

"So," Benny phonated, peeking over the silver rims of his circular glasses, "what's it gon' be?"

A spindly, deep brown grandfather clock chimed in the corner of the room; it's long hand on twelve and the shorter on three.

"Retirement don't pay debts," Al brought up, "and we got *plenty* of debts to pay."

Desmond sat up, watching the men. "If we do this job," he said, tolerantly, "I presume we're done with Mister Galvani?"

"God, I hope so," added Carson. "That bastard is trouble for us."

"Yeah, we *will* be," said Al, rubbing his eye and meddling with his empty whiskey glass.

"Where is this train, anyway?" Houston questioned before crossing his arms.

"It's a freight train. And like I said, I don't know much. *But* all I know is that it's in Crown Summit."

Reese perked up. "That's where Galvani lives. Up north, by the mountains."

"He does," Al agreed.

"Then I'm sure he's more than capable of doing it himself," said Reese, stretching his arms.

"What'd I'd say a moment ago, Reese?" huffed Al, sliding his glass to the side.

"What about *this* train? What's it got that's worth stealin'?" asked Benny, curiously. "Must be haulin' somethin' interestin'."

Once more, Al raised himself out of the chair, bending his

worn-out knees and loosening his shoulders. "I'm gonna have a word with Mister Galvani. We'll be arrangin' a meeting, so he'll explain everything. To me, at least."

"And we can trust him?" prest Benny.

"We ain't got no choice," Al responded. "We owe him *big time*. Need I remind you; you know what he's capable of, don't you? We can't risk this."

A short laugh lasting only a few breaths emerged from Benny. "Looks like we're back in business, gentlemen."

The wintry afternoon had become a grayish blue shroud, and the clouds fell as if they were kissing the ground, submerging the manor and landscape in deep fog. Empty glasses were placed at the center of the wide table and their elbows resting on its curved edges. A reflection bounced from the table's polished surface from the dangling silver chandelier above, splitting into five arcs and illuminating the small room with sandy light.

Al tugged the hefty curtains and blocked out the murky mist.

"I guess we're all in, King" said Benny, watching the men and then glaring at Al.

"One more job. That's it," Al specified.

Admittedly, they all shook their heads, but no words slipped.

"Benny and Desmond," stated Al, rising from the table, "you're both with me when the time comes for the meetin'."

"Yes, sir," said Desmond, agreeingly.

"All right," Benny made clear, standing up and walking toward the pretty door. "This better be worth it."

His hand patted and turned the shiny doorknob, and he

pulled the door open, stepping into the hallway of children.

"Uncle Benny!" yelled a pint-sized girl.

Benny peaked down and smiled at her little face. "Have you been behavin'?"

"*Have you been behavin'?*" she mocked him before giggling.

Her giggles became louder when Benny threw the girl into the air, catching her tiny body when she fell.

"Lunch is ready," her joyous screams remarked. "I was coming to tell you all."

Her boots had trodden over the carpet, creating miniature craters as she went.

"No runnin' in the house, young lady," said Benny, watching her descend the pale stairs.

Soon enough, his heavy fist thundered against the door, and he called out to the rest. "Fellas, time to eat!"

Discreetly, Otis approached Benny from behind, startling him with his crimped hand patting his shoulder. Benny returned with an irate glance. The door had opened, and Carson stepped into the hallway, noting Otis.

"My boy, Carson!" said Otis, excitedly. "It's been too long. At least you'll have *some* respect for me, unlike these fools."

The door was held ajar, and Carson nodded his head, mumbling to himself, "Oh, Lord, not him," then entered the room again.

"You're quite the celebrity!" Benny laughed.

"I'm surrounded by a bunch of jerks," Otis uttered, throwing his hand around. Reese pranced into the hallway shortly after.

"Reese," Otis put forth; his eyes tailing the man marching away.

"Oh, dear God," Reese whispered to himself and voyaged down the stairs.

"Let's eat, Otis," declared Benny, guiding the older man to the landing. "Careful on the stairs, buddy. We don't want to send you to back to Missus McDonough in bits."

The dining room was perky; knee-high youngsters ran around in their boots, dodging the furniture and screaming at one another. Their fathers joining in on the fun, too!

"Settle down, children!" Caroline called from the toasty kitchen, readying the dinner plates and silver cutlery.

The scent was prodigious, filling the kitchen in a warm and tasty blanket. Fooling with the children, the men sat at the table and amused the little ones.

"Hope you got your sweet teeth ready!" Valentine trumpeted, hauling in the food with the men's wives, followed by Sloane.

They gently placed trays in the center of the long, brindle table; steam rising off the grandiose dinner. The sugar-glazed ham looked lavish, and the honey-glazed carrots glittered in its pot. Mashed potatoes dominated a green bowl, like a heap of snow, and a vegetable stew swam in a large casserole.

"Damn, you've outdone yourselves, again, ladies!" Al imparted, delightfully.

"Language at the table, hon," said Caroline, who was placing the heated dinner plates and cutlery onto the table.

Silently, the children sat beside their parents, peering at the sweltering food and waiting for their mothers and fathers to crane a piece onto their plates. Cups of rich, fruity orange juice were prepared for the devious children, while the adults mixed theirs with gin or vodka, or wine was an option, too.

THOSE LUCKY FELLAS: PART 1

What else would stop them from losing their minds?

"The recipe was my idea," said Valentine, "but Sloane helped me cook it."

Benny smiled at her sinless face. "This was the *surprise* you mentioned earlier?"

"Sure is, Mister Falcon."

"Looks incredible!" he said proudly. "Well done to you, too, Sloane."

She took a seat beside Valentine; her mouth stretching from ear to ear. "Thank you, Benny."

Keenly, the family dug into their meals, tearing through the sparkling ham and biting into the gloopy carrots. The boiling vegetable stew was poured onto the side of their plates, and the children were warned to let it cool.

A succulent scent encased the open dining room, as the cutlery pierced and pecked at the meal and as always, compliments were thrown toward the ladies. Otis sipped on his strong whiskey. It was sufficient to keep him awake—most of the time. He would make-believe with his food; making little people or cubes with the mashed potatoes to show off to the children for the purpose of hearing their giggles.

Caroline teemed the last droplets of vegetable soup onto her plate, which by now must have been cold. "How'd the meeting go, darling?" she asked Al.

"Good," he said, swallowing his last bite.

"What did you discuss?" she felt out, placing the empty casserole bowl onto the side.

"Not much. Just... *work*. The usual stuff," Al addressed. "Nothin' to worry about, Caroline. The stew was delicious, hon."

She brought a bright look. "Thank you, darling."

When the final bits of food were swallowed, their drinks had washed their mouths, feeling refreshed. Methodically, the women carried the dishes into the kitchen and the children scooted into the living room.

Al stood from the table and walked into the white hallway. "Benny, come with me, son," he proposed.

"One more road trip, I suppose," Benny remarked, burping into his fist and shuffled himself into the hallway.

"I gotta make a call with Galvani," said Al faintly, taking a glimpse over his shoulder.

"What d'ya need me for, Boss? You have your own car," Benny alleged.

"We ain't gon' make a call *here*," Al weighed in, nodding his head. "I'll need you to drive me to a nearby telephone."

A long sigh emanated from Benny. "Sure. Whatever you say."

"Won't be too long, Mister Falcon," Al said, blithely.

At once, they departed and Al turned his head around the door frame, peering into what was now a noiseless dining room.

"Forget somethin'," Benny soughed.

"We'll be back soon. Stay here, gentleman. And behave yourselves," said Al.

With his crinkly fingers, he waved a two-finger salute and directed himself toward the dainty front doors.

"Let's go, Boss," Benny declared, slipping into his black woolly coat.

Al fetched his coat from the closet and garbed himself in his, too, then followed Benny into the divine front yard and they drew closer to the Hudson Hornet.

Its silver key turned in the frigid lock and clicked. The two hunkered onto the chilly leather seat and Benny slid the key into the ignition; its engine triggered, and the exhaust brayed. The headlights purged through the dense fog, enough to see what lay ahead.

"You armed?" Al enquired.

"Sure am," said Benny, revealing his favorite Colt M1911A1 pistol holstered under his left arm.

"Good," Al bounced back. "Worry not, I am, too," he added, revealing an immaculate silver Colt New Service revolver and pointed to a small engraving; *The King* it read by the moon clip.

"You like that? Just picked it up this mornin'." chuckled Mister King.

"It's pointless," said Benny, laughing at Al. "No one's gon' see it, Boss, 'specially when it's *that* tiny."

"That's not the point," garbled Al, sluggishly holstering the pistol under his arm, then stared blindly into the fog. "Get goin', Mister Falcon."

Unexpectedly, a thwack erupted on the window, startling both Benny and Al.

"Jeez!" Benny winced, lowering the thin glass.

"Hey, fellas!" Otis stated, kneeling through the gap. "You mind if an old friend joins ya?" he requested, cladded in a light brown overcoat and matching flat cap.

"'Course not. *If* you open the gate. I forgot to do that," Al supposed.

"I'll do that," said Otis, excitedly, ambulating toward the broad gate.

"All right, fine," stammered Benny, rolling over the driveway and through the spacious opening, before stopping for the cranky old man.

"Should I drive off?" Benny chortled.

Al shook his head, smiling.

Clangs heaved from the gate and once it was secured, Otis perched onto the seat in the back of the Hudson Hornet.

"You got a gun with ya, Mister McDonough?" asked Benny.

"Why'd I need that?" he replied, straightening his crooked back.

"You got one or not?" Al broached before turning his head toward Otis.

"No, I ain't got one on me," said Otis.

Benny was hesitant, even as he removed his leather holster from under his arm with his pistol stocked within and commended it to Otis, who snagged it, pleasurably.

"You remember how to use it, *right*?" asked Benny, sounding troubled.

"I know how to use it, dummy. I *was* in the military, remember?" Otis heralded.

"Good riddance, he ain't gonna shoot us," Benny stifled to Al.

"Once you're done with your little *tea party*, we can get goin'," groaned Al, resting his shivering cheek on his fist and his bony elbow against the door.

"Take these, old man," said Benny, reaching into his long coat's inner silky pocket and handing over two full magazines; seven bullets in each.

"Not sayin' we'll *need* guns, but it's a good idea to have 'em,"

THOSE LUCKY FELLAS: PART 1

Al pitched, moving his head away from Otis' reach.

"Watch and learn," said Otis, stashing the magazines into a deep side pocket. "I'll show you how it's done."

Chapter Fourteen

Big Iron

Heedfully, the mud-stained tires swiveled down the cloudy drive and only a few feet of the road ahead were visible; a mire road leading away from the manor. The sun began to dip below the horizon, painting the sky with faint hues of yellow and orange and casting a warm glow over Knox.

When they drove around an uneven, hilly bend, an unpleasant gritting noise was noted from underneath the Hudson Hornet.

"Easy, boy," said Otis, clutching tightly onto the seat in front of him.

"I'm countin' on you to get us there in one piece," Al divulged, peeking over at the grumpy man.

"Yeah, I know that," said Benny, worriedly, "I just don't understand why we gotta take *these* roads out of town," he put forth, further wrestling his eyes with the haunting fog.

"It's safe," Al supposed, finding it difficult to concentrate with his eyepatch itching his eye socket. "Well... *safer*. It's also the closest telephone to us."

Gradually, the fog had seemed to become thinner, unearthing a pickup truck following them closely from behind.

"Anyone see that car before?" Benny declared, glaring at its headlights sparkle into the door mirror.

"How long d'ya think they've been followin' us?" said Al, peering over the seat behind him.

"No clue, King," said Otis, turning around, "I ain't seen them 'til now."

THOSE LUCKY FELLAS: PART 1

The sonorous sound of the six cylinders faded when the Hudson Hornet halted beside an isolated timber post office, overtopping the calm sea.

"Pull up over there," said Al, pointing to the side of the road. "I'll use the telephone here."

Benny drew the heavy car to a halt by the crammed building and switched off the headlights before cutting the engine. The pickup truck had driven by, vanishing into the louring fog. A sharp silence had struck them and the door opened.

"Wait here, gentleman. And keep an eye out," Al prompted, advancing toward the tiny post office and slamming the door behind him.

His heels skated across the floor and clanged onto the wooden steps. Benny yawned bluntly, straightened his elbows and stretched his arms upward, accidentally thudding the clothed roof. Otis, silently, yawned behind him.

"If Al came all this way to use a telephone, then it's *serious*," Otis averred. "What're you morons gettin' yourselves into this time?"

"Hey, just sit there. Stay quiet, man."

Finding it difficult to stay awake, Otis played with his tongue, flicking it around his dry mouth.

Benny watched Al in the rear-view mirror wave his hand and spit words into the telephone, but he could not make out if he was agitated.

Unexpectedly, a pickup truck hurled across the road and its tires screeched when it braked, alarming the two, and became almost invisible when its lights were cut.

"What in God's name..." mumbled Otis, looking into the fog through narrowed eyes.

"This don't look good," Benny said worryingly. "It's that same damn truck that was followin' us. I ain't seen folk like them before," he appended, staring at two men leave the dented vehicle and stroll toward them.

"Wait here," he whispered to Otis and hurriedly opened his door, moving toward the back of the Hudson Hornet.

Covertly, he upheaved the trunk and checked the magazine of his Browning Automatic Rifle; almost full, he noticed.

"Amigos," Benny greeted the visitors, with his right hand tucked away, grasping the rifle that lay in the big trunk. "You were followin' us closely back there. What's that all about?"

"We couldn't see your car, *friend*," replied one of the strangers, as the other approached the post office and entered. Benny nodded, densely.

"What's your business here, at this time?" Benny pressed, but before he could receive an answer, a loud bang arose from the post office and an injured man toppled through the door; his body hammering the wood when he fell.

"Benny!" Al barked. "Start the car!"

Before Benny could dig out his rifle, the man who stood before him drew a pistol, but was shot in his head by Otis.

"Don't let 'em draw first, Benny!" the old man gabbled, as more rusty and partially damaged vehicles reached a standstill on the road.

Benny lugged his dearest rifle and crouched behind his car.

"You think it's those farmers?" yelped Al, kneeling behind an old mail truck and peeping from behind.

"Comstocks? Can't be! We killed 'em!" Benny shouted back, ducking and firing at the threat.

He hunkered over the front of the Hudson Hornet, aiming

his firearm and firing a round, then sprung up and fired a few more.

Bodies had scattered the road and bullet holes decorated the vehicles; pickup trucks and saloons, mostly. The deafening sound of the gunshots was unpleasant, but it was about to get worse.

"Son of a bitch!" Otis sneered, dropping the pistol by his foot and clung onto a wound on his right shoulder. "Goddammit!" he shouted, wrapping his cockled fingers tighter over the wound, yet blood poured down his arm, like a stream.

"Stay there, Otis!" cawed Al, stepping out from the side of the mail truck and gunning down the men.

It was quiet when Benny killed the last man that cowered in the fog. He pointed the rifle upward, leaning it against his shoulder and held Otis with his left.

"You're gon' be fine, buddy," he said, seeing Al plod over. "Luckily, the weather was on our side."

"I'm dyin', man," Otis replied with his eyes squeezed together.

"Don't give me hope," Benny mumbled.

Al holstered his revolver and dipped beside Otis, lifting him by his arm. "Come now, Otis, you'll be fine. Missus King will get you patched up when we get back."

The door was thrown wide enough to get the sobbing old man through.

"I ain't gonna make it," Otis hushed.

"Calm down, Otis," Benny declared, "it's just a scratch."

"You ain't the one that's been shot!" shouted Otis, crawling into the rear of the car and roosting onto the plushy seat.

With prudence, Al tied a handkerchief to his bony arm.

"Settle down. Let me tie this to ya."

Benny snapped up his pistol from the frosty asphalt, handing it slowly to Otis, and then placed his rifle beside him. "Hold on to this and don't drop it this time."

"Let's get home quick," Al proposed, settling distressfully into the front beside Benny. "If they'd come for us, then I worry about the rest back at home."

"Do you think they were Peacekeepers?" Benny wondered.

"Can't be. They don't be dressin' like *that*. And they definitely don't just open fire without talkin' first!"

"You said they might be Comstocks?" Otis chimed in.

"Impossible. They're dead," said Benny, "and they don't dress like those fuckers, either. Not *that bad*, anyway."

A collection of faint muffles was made clear from behind their seat, which grew silent when the engine was set in motion; clattering through the trees. Groaning came from Otis, who closed his eyes and tried his best to ignore the pain.

Soon, the Hudson Hornet hurried, pouncing and slewing through the country roads, whirling dust into the air and twirling the fog as the black car ploughed on.

"Almost there, Otis, hang on," Al reassured, kindly.

"It's gettin' cold," Otis muttered, "and my head... It feels... light."

"I can saw off your arm... if that'll help," Benny said, patiently, clearing his throat.

He reached into his inner pocket and ejected a leather cigar case made from pigskin. The flap was lifted from its little strap and Benny used his spotless teeth to extract the vanilla cigar from the case, which had already been cut. After a while, the mouthwatering scent of strong vanilla and burning tobacco filled the car.

"Mister McDonough!" Benny belled. "Here, smoke this," he reached out, holding the butt of the cigar. "You'll feel better. And it *should* keep you from whinin'."

Otis gripped the cigar between his thumb and index finger and rested it between his tattered lips, inhaling it every so often. The constant petulance traded with unwavering coughing when resting his forehead against his palm. Bustling over the roads and splitting through the fog caused Otis to complain more, but they had to hurry!

"Don't think about it too much," Benny put forth, looking in all directions; the road, Otis and his mirrors. "It'll be over soon... Once we take that bullet out. Oh, and what happened with the conversation, Boss?"

Al looked over at Benny. "Galvani wants to meet and talk more. In person, obviously. Little bastard refused to have the conversation over the phone. Anyway, I'll tell you all when we get back."

They were getting close to home, shifting through sparse country roads with rolling hills stretched out on either side.

The anxious old man fidgeted in his seat, still pressing his wound. "You think they're followin us?"

"Ain't nobody followin' us," said Al, grouchily, but his annoyance was not aimed at the men. "We killed 'em back there, they ain't comin'. They better not be."

A wintery evening air rushed in through the open windows and petted their faces.

"Feels good, don't it? Steady breaths, now," said Benny, heartily and to no surprise, Otis responded with more grunts.

With the brakes whistling, the Hudson Hornet came to a

sudden stop and the small rocks along the road caused the car to jostle and bounce. Benny would have refrained from a harsh stop, but the odd vehicles stationed on the rough road and the dreadful screams made his heart turn to stone.

"Those fuckin' bastards are *here*!" said Al, opening his door.

Grabbing his rifle from the behind him, Benny bailed out and hid behind his door, pulling the trigger and firing at two figures moving through the ghostly fog.

"Keep your head down, Otis!" Benny shouted, pacing toward the manor and listening to the obnoxious sound of more gunfire.

"Benny, I'm right behind ya!" Al bellowed, leaving the car in a hurry, too.

"Watch your fire, boys!" Al blustered. "We're comin' from the path!"

There was silence, and it was not long before a few shots echoed again. Bodies sprawled beside the cars. The stillness had returned after the shells plummeted onto the soil and Benny and Al crept over to the drive of the manor, joining up with Houston and Desmond.

"Hold ya fire!" hailed Benny.

"What in the world is goin' on?" said Houston, lowering his shotgun.

Dipping his head, Al wiped his nose. "I'll explain once we're done with *this*," pointing at the mess behind them.

"Everyone all right?" said Benny, composedly.

"Thankfully," Desmond answered, panting.

Strolling along the drive came Carson, carrying a rifle over his shoulder and Reese clenching a pistol in his hand.

"What the fuck just happened?" Carson posed. "They

came to the house. That ain't good, man."

"Everyone is fine. *That's* good, at least," said Al.

"Hey, don't let Otis hear that," Benny chuckled.

"Any idea who they were?" asked Reese, finding a need to add to the conversation.

"Pro'ly thieves," said Benny. "And if it ain't *thieves*, then I ain't got a clue. They attacked us before. When we was out."

Al walked through the crowd, holstering his precious revolver. "We'll talk about it when we're inside. And, Benny," he said, swiveling, "be sure to grab Otis."

"I forgot about that," he sighed.

Benny tripped over to his car and faintly deplored when peering at the scratches on the chrome bumper.

"Benny?" Otis gasped.

"What's it now?"

The door opened and Otis leaned against his seat with his shoulders slumped. "You're gon' have to carry me, man. It hurts," he whined.

Benny's eyebrows furrowed and his eyes turned blank. "Get out the damn car, Otis," he hissed, tucking onto his arm and levering him out.

The old man shrieked, "Watch it!"

As they both stood, the door was flung shut and Benny's lips were tightly pressed and his jaw was tense.

"Hey, man, why so aggressive?" Otis whined, as usual.

"Have you *seen* the car?" said Benny bitterly. "Look at the state of her. I just got her cleaned and now she's a mess! And it's all *your* fault."

Otis was baffled. "My fault?"

"Yes, *yours*... and Al's," Benny scoffed, setting out for the house. "Better haul your ass up to the house and see Caroline."

They scaled the hill beside one another and Otis made short chuffs as he ascended, tightly holding onto his wound with his blood-stained fingers. Benny was surprised that Otis managed to retreat to the house despite his constant complaining, but it was not long before he became bothersome again.

The men caught a glimpse of the two.

"What the hell happened out there?" Desmond avouched, stomping along the path.

"What happened to *you*?" asked Carson, glaring at Otis' bloodied arm.

"What's it look like, dummy?" he spat back. "This is Benny's doin'. He don't have a clue how to fight."

"Hey, I ain't the one that's been shot, remember?" said Benny, smirking. "I thought you was in the military."

Otis sighed deeply. "I *was* in the military," he said in a sharp tone.

"You sure about that?" Benny chuckled.

Carson bumped Otis on his bony shoulder and laughed. "That's a bit of a stretch," he said.

As usual, Otis raised his voice, "I *was*! You bastards gave me a cold welcome and now you're laughin' after I've been shot!"

"Feels like the good old days, don't it?" Benny hooted with laughter. "You're like a little puppy we gotta take care of, or you'll go bitin' everyone on the ankles."

They all laughed, taking no notice of Otis.

Desmond rested his hand on his shoulder and said, "Otis, buddy, we've had worse."

"Anyway, we gon' move them cars or what?" Houston said, pointing toward the end of the path with a flick of his finger.

THOSE LUCKY FELLAS: PART 1

Al returned to the front yard, treading through the thin fog, and Caroline followed, wailing at the group. "Whatever you bastards did out there, you've put us *all* in *danger*! Could've gotten us *all* killed! Have some decency for once! Fools! All of ya!"

A heavy silence filled the air.

"Shut your mouth, silly woman," Al announced sternly. "And, here..." he stomped over to Otis and hooked him by the arm, "take him and patch him up. That bullet needs to be taken out."

Soon, the sound of a nimble stampede left the manor and became harsher when it reached the fancy water fountain. It was Sloane and Valentine, and their dresses shimmered in the setting sun.

"What're ya doin' out here? Get back inside, both of you!" Benny called, fluttering his hand.

"Nobody comes out tonight," Al instilled, and as a result, Caroline immediately assisted Otis to the manor.

"Let's get goin'," Benny declared, falling back to the vehicles that occupied the dirt road.

It was not long before the jarring sound of tires stabbing into the dirt was made clear.

"Great... Now what?" Al whispered to himself.

Two familiar faces were coming their way; faces the men did not like nor want to see. And even worse, their hideous dark gray suits.

"Vulpes," Benny greeted him with a low swish in his voice.

"Evening, gentlemen," he asserted, cradling his shotgun in his arms. "Caught you in the act, did I not?"

The air filled with stillness and Al stood in front of his men, towering over the two visitors.

"And what might that *act* be?" said Al, itching his brow above his eyepatch.

Vulpes pivoted toward the way he came. "You see those cars? Those dead men? They *are* outside of your... *lovely* home. Those gunshots were heard for miles. You mind telling me what's going on?"

"That aint—" but Benny was cut off by Vulpes' bitterness.

"*I* did not ask you *anything*, mister. Not *yet*."

At once, Benny loomed over Vulpes, and this was no surprise to the gang.

"Don't, son," Al advised and pushed his hand forward.

"You listen to me, boy!" Benny started to blare, and he raised his chin. "You Peacekeepers were *never* welcomed to Knox," Benny began to thunder, "and since you've been here, there's been nothin' but more *chaos* for us *all* to endure. So..." he stepped closer to Vulpes, "you better watch who you're fuckin' talkin' to. You understand me?"

Benny leaned back, breathing in heavy breaths to calm himself.

Vulpes' eyes widened and his mouth unlatched. "If that's your opinion, then so be it. But I asked what happened."

"To be honest, we don't know ourselves. We're not evil people," Al said, squinting a little. "Way I see it, we was just defending our home."

In no hurry, Vulpes handed his speckless shotgun over to his partner and clung to a pair of shiny handcuffs. "Go and clear that mess," he ordered the gang, but they stood like rocks. "Mister King, step forward. Don't make this difficult for me," he said, reaching out into the empty.

THOSE LUCKY FELLAS: PART 1

Al drew nearer to Vulpes with his hands out. "Be my guest," he said, smiling coldly.

Vulpes felt his legs stiffen when he heard the grating sound of guns clicking and saw the older men lifting their firearms in the corner of his eyes.

"Do not do anything stupid. I urge you all to reconsider your decisions," Vulpes stated, dropping his hands and stowing away the handcuffs.

"You're a wise man," Al said, patting him on the shoulder, but Vulpes began to step away, dodging Al's big hand.

"You are all misguided and, someday, your consequences will help you realize the day you crossed us. I am making it as easy as I can for you all. We Peacekeepers may be ruthless and cruel, but it is for the greater good, gentlemen, because we seek to bring order, to create a society of honest men and women. And those who refuse to adapt will disappear... like the rest."

"*Like the rest?*" Benny repeated.

"The rest of the scum plaguing this land," Vulpes scoffed.

With the current situation in mind, Vulpes soundly gripped his shotgun, tipped his head and herded his partner toward the end of the path.

"That dumbass has got guts, I'll give him that," Al uttered, resting a hand on his hip.

Without hurry, Vulpes rotated and waved. "Gentlemen, the next time we meet, I will be bringing *more* men with me," he called, and the two disappeared over the fence.

"Good riddance," Al mumbled. "Fellas, get those cars off the road. And I called Donato and Diego to take them away."

"When did ya do that?" said Benny, puzzled.

"Before the wife startin' yellin'," Al riposted.

"To where?" Reese wondered.

"What's it matter?" Carson replied, nudging him on his back.

Houston followed and peeked over his shoulder. "Let's go, Desmond," he said.

"Very well," Desmond countered, accompanying the rest.

Tepidly, Al lazed his hand on Benny's shoulder and stood by his side. "You go on ahead, my boy. I'll have a word with the ladies. Try calmin' them down."

Benny departed. "Good luck, Boss. They're gon' eat us all alive if you don't. Best take their minds off it."

The cars that appeared earlier, now somewhat wrecked, seemed old, and the men noticed the rust beginning to emerge. Not only were the windows cracked, but the paint was chipped with orange and brown blotches. And as for the bodies, the overalls and buttoned shirts appeared to be tatty and in need of repair, with fading colors and frayed edges.

Desmond had cautiously lifted a pistol from the ground. "These guns are just as rickety as their cars. Have you seen the *state* of these?" he said, picking up a ruined bolt-action rifle and stockpiling it into the cargo bed of a decaying pickup truck with the other faulty firearms.

"They gotta be thieves," said Houston, quickly, carefully moving a corpse into the trunk of another tarnished car.

"Or bounty hunters," Carson included, lending a hand.

"We don't have a bounty on our heads, but you could be right," said Reese, joining in with the others.

"Amigos! You made it!" Benny delightfully yelled at the sight of Diego and Donato rolling over a hill from behind the disarray.

THOSE LUCKY FELLAS: PART 1

They were pleased to see him, too.

"Mister King needed us to move some stuff, but we didn't expect this mess, my friend!" Donato snickered, parting from his car, and Diego followed, waving at the gang.

"This *mess* needs clearing, obviously," said Benny, "and you folks are the best choice we got."

"Yes, sir, but where do you want it?" returned Donato.

"Anywhere but not *here*," Benny replied, whilst pointing at the license plates. "These have gotta go. It don't matter what you do with the cars and the guns, just get rid of the bodies and the license plates."

Both Spanish men nodded.

"Think you can handle it?"

They nodded again and shook hands with Benny, and Diego spoke merrily, but Benny did not understand a word.

"What did he say?" he sought an answer.

Donato translated, "He said we owe you gentlemen everything. You helped us out and now let us return the favor."

"It's a good thing we're on the same page this time and not almost blowin' each other's brains out," Benny laughed. "Hey, fellas," he implored to his men, "give 'em a hand," then strolled back to the bottom of the hill to his Hudson Hornet and tried his best to not stare at the damage, but he already did and sighed heavily.

The tires spun when Benny drove up the hill and slipped by the pools of blood, then navigated to the water fountain in the front yard. When the engine was cut and the delightful sound of singing birds returned, Benny attempted to clear his mind, but the damage to his car was stapled into his thoughts that he had even forgotten about the whole trip to begin with.

"Mister Falcon," said Carson, opening the car's black door, "have you seen the damage to the other side?

Painfully, Benny agreed, slowly nodding his head.

"Can you fix it? I mean, it just needs a lick of paint, that's all," said Benny.

"Sure, of course, brother. Let me take it to town tomorrow and she'll be ready in a few days."

Carson backed up when Benny left the car and handed him the silver keys.

In the corner of his eyes, Benny glanced at Diego and Donato, prepping for a departure. "Leavin' already?" he yelled across the drive.

"We'll be making a few trips to get it all out, Mister Falcon," Donato shouted back, waving with his dirty brown hat in hand.

"Muchas gracias, amigo," cheered Donato, and the pickup truck repelled from the dirt road.

Benny waved farewell and faced Carson. "I need to talk to Al," he said, advancing toward the floral front doors of the manor. "Keep an eye on 'em, Carson."

A great deal of uproar enraged throughout the manor the moment Benny entered, but it was Otis' wailing that dominated the rest, even the loud shrieks from the crying children felt quiet. Benny rubbed his eyes from under his glasses and was startled when he saw Al standing before him.

"About that phone call with Mister Galvani," said Al, clicking his fingers twice, "he wants to meet with us next week. Saturday, just after sunrise. To discuss the train job, of course."

Miserably, Benny focused on Al. "We're *really* goin' through with this? After what just happened?"

"Like I said earlier, we ain't got no choice. We owe him," Al flung back. "We're *goin'* next Saturday."

"Fine, but who's goin'?"

Al's dark brown eyes darted to Benny's. "You, me, and someone else. Who're ya thinkin'?"

Benny, dourly, switched his rifle to his left hand. "I say we take Desmond," he said earnestly. "He's great with words and knows how to discuss matters. Wait a minute... You said it was the two of us when the time comes. You forget about that?"

Al yawned and wiped his watery eye. "Yeah, I remember now, Mister Falcon. I shall inform him tomorrow."

"Where are we meetin' Lloyd?"

Turning around, Al looked at Benny. "Remember Silver Springs? The small town up north?"

"Yeah, I remember that old dump," said Benny, rattily; the words spitting from his mouth. "Why'd you choose *there*? Could've had the meetin' anywhere else, you know. Somewhere closer to home."

Al stood at the bottom of the staircase and turned his head. "Exactly! We'll be *far* from home, and it's a little town. Ain't nobody gonna be lookin' for us over there." He turned around and ascended the stairs, digging his feet into the soft carpet. "Oh, and we can pick out a souvenir!" he laughed.

Benny brushed his hair with his fingers. "Nobody goes to Silver Springs," he muttered and steered himself into the living room, where, finally, the women and children had simmered down.

"Everyone okay?" said Benny comfortingly. Not a single word was spoken, but their heads bowed. "We're safe now. I got rid of the bad guys. We'll watch a movie tonight, how 'bout that? What was it... Treasure Island?" he said, reassuring the children and left the comfortable room with a warm smile.

It was not too long before Caroline pursued Benny into the entrance hall, stomping her heels before him. "Mister Falcon," she stormed, "what is wrong with you? A movie... after what just happened? You men brought this onto us, so stop actin' like everythin' seems fine!"

Rolling his eyes, Benny glared at the woman. "Tell you what," Benny grumbled and handed over his rifle to Caroline, "take this and use it when you *need* it."

With a sharp glare, Caroline stepped backward. "Don't be a damn fool, boy! Guns aren't a lady's thing."

The rifle slept in Benny's arms again and he tittered, "I thought so, Missus King," he said firmly, and reached for the beautiful white staircase. "I thought so."

His bedroom door gleamed as the soft light had shunned onto its warm walnut and painted the hallway with a gracious orange glow.

Benny was exhausted, and upon entering his motionless bedroom, he let out a deep sigh of relief. The gentle scent of vanilla had calmed him and he rested his rifle against the oak wardrobe, extracting its magazine and helping himself to a shot of sweet whiskey.

Gingerly, he swept the flavorful liquid around his mouth and felt it warm his body when he swallowed. It was a longing kick he needed after a bizarre and tiresome day.

Chapter Fifteen

Still Waters Run Deep

Saturday had arrived. Benny stared at the morning sun expanding over the horizon and daubing the sky with tones of orange and pink, and had high hopes that today would be finer. A fine film of frost dusted the ground, and the world seemed to be enveloped in serenity.

Benny towered above the edge of the cliff and his eyes shifted to the sea, observing the calm water. The regular waves were absent and thus the ocean displayed the sky, like a face in a mirror. In the distance, the silhouette of Boston's skyline nestled.

To wake up before the rest was a strange feeling, Benny thought, as it was usually the cheer and the joy from the children that would wake him, or Sloane would drag him out of bed if he slept for too long. Still, the solitude was pleasant.

The door's thick latch opened and out came Al, rubbing together his bare hands and adjusting his black fedora. "Good mornin', Mister Falcon. Are ya ready?" he said eagerly, pushing his dry hands into a pair of black leather gloves.

It was remarkable... Al *hated* meetings.

But why was he so happy?

"Mornin' to ya, too, Boss," said Benny, facing the happy man.

"Lovely morning, ain't it?" Desmond expressed, heading toward his parked car; a black 1949 Dodge Coronet, and twisted the key inside the lock.

"It sure is, Mister Kane," Al answered, taking a seat beside Desmond in the front.

"Save the talkin' for when we get there," Benny voiced just after opening the gate. "Go on through and wait for me."

The gate clinked, and Benny made himself snug in the back seats—almost lying on them—relaxing his tense shoulders and neck. Desmond set off, and they ventured over the endless ribbon of twists and turns, over the open country roads and climbed steep hills. Benny stuck his hand between the side of his holster. The constant bumping of the pistol agitated him.

Once they had broken away from the west and had ditched the bumpy roads, a delightful stretch of smooth asphalt cut through the snowy mountains. Tall, slender spruce trees slept on both sides of the road and the view was pretty.

"We ain't got much to go," said Al, glaring at his silver pocket watch. "I don't know about you two, but I am *starving*."

Desmond looked over at Al. "It's been almost an hour since we left home. You really *that* hungry?"

"Let's stop for some donuts when we get into town," he said, then twisted around to find Benny rustling a bag of jelly beans.

"What?" questioned Benny, nibbling a few of the juicy, flavorful treats. He leisurely tilted the bag toward Al. "Have some, they're good."

"No, thank you," Al stated. "Jelly beans are childish."

Benny jerked up. "Hey, look," he said, adamantly, "jelly beans are the *best* thing that happened to America."

He shuffled the bag near Desmond, but he declined.

"Somethin' is wrong with you all," Benny whispered and leaned back again.

The sunlight flickered through the wide gaps between the trees as the car flew over the glistening road. An old voice spoke through the radio; it seems like the next few days would be clear, thankfully.

"We finally made it, boys," said Al, peering at the grand sign by the side of the road; *Welcome to Silver Springs!*

The small town rested against the shore of the untouched lake. Wooden docks stretched out and suspended over the calm water, and charming stores were lined along the clean streets. Sloping hills sat behind the town and were dotted with more lush spruce trees, though the tallest object was the magnificent clock tower rising from the center of the town; nine o'clock. The staggering chime echoed across the streets, provoking the birds to take flight.

"Park her here," Al prompted, pointing at a corner of a tiny building. "Dunkin' Donuts... what's that?" he whispered, staring at the burnished sign. The car stopped, and the engine switched off.

"We're getting donuts from here, Boss?" asked Desmond.

"It says *donuts*, so let's go. You comin', Benny?"

Before Al could turn around, Benny was already on his feet. "I thought you was in the mood for donuts," he said.

"I am," Al replied, leaving the warmth of the car behind.

"You sure are takin' your sweet time," Benny mumbled, chuckling to himself.

"Shut up, Benny," said Al, sighing and walking to the store.

As he tugged at the door, opening it for a lady and a child, the succulent aroma of freshly baked donuts spouted toward him and the scent made his mouth water. "Dear God," Al whispered.

The bright creamy walls were lined with framed photographs and the overhead lights caused the sugary glaze to glow. A cheerful voice had greeted the men, and they galloped toward the glass counter.

"Good morning, gentlemen," said a pretty woman. "What would you like?"

Al was delighted. "Mornin', ma'am. Could we have…" he turned toward Benny and Desmond, then back at the lady, "six glazed donuts, please?"

"Yes, sir," she said, softly. "And would you fellas like any coffee? You can *dunk* your donuts," she laughed, and the men laughed, too!

"Why not?" Al grinned and paid the woman, who handed back his change.

"Take a seat and I'll bring them right out," she twinkled, roving into the kitchen.

Thrilled, the three flumped onto the cushy circular stools by the counter and as for the rest of the restaurant, it was vacant with only a clock ticking and a muted luminous jukebox occupying one corner.

In a tick, the waitress gracefully stepped forward and planted a plate of six hot donuts on the counter; six sparkling rings. "Here you are, fellas. Dig in!" she said cheerfully.

"Thank you, darling," Al remarked, lifting a soft, fluffy donut.

"And here is your coffee," said the waitress, pouring the steaming liquid into three speckless white mugs. The donuts were ripped, then dipped into the blistering coffee and they quickly devoured them before the sugary glazing had melted entirely.

"Damn, this stuff is *real* good!" said Al, warming his hands onto the side of his mug.

THOSE LUCKY FELLAS: PART 1

"Better than I hoped," Desmond stated, licking the sugar on his thumb.

"Tell you what, that was great," said Benny. "But imagine jelly beans on a donut."

The waitress laughed, but the other two sighed.

"Listen, if you had my idea, this place wouldn't be so devoid," Benny laughed at the waitress. "Ma'am, you tell the guy who runs this place there's a man wantin' to propose a brilliant idea."

She giggled and bit her red lip. "I will, sir."

"Don't be ridiculous, Benny," Al maundered and stood up from his stool, tilting his head at the waitress.

"Leaving already, gentlemen?" she said, calmly.

"We gotta get to work, ma'am," said Desmond. "Thank you for your service and have a wonderful day."

"Same goes for you fellas and thank you, again," she hurled back.

Benny left a tip on the counter and followed Al, bidding farewell to the waitress and leaving the homely restaurant. Despite the biting, smallish winds, the sun remained and Silver Springs had been buried in golden rays. Even though the meeting would take place by the docks—down the road from the restaurant—they insisted on moving the car.

Once Desmond had parked on the street, the men withdrew and walked over to the docks, crunching over the frost beneath them. Benny had not felt the sand when he plodded onto the beach, as it was completely frozen and only realized when he looked down. Toward the end of the wide dock, where the meeting would come about, a set of white plastic chairs tarried in a circle, but there was no sign of Galvani.

Al sulked and said, "He ain't even here," to Benny and Desmond, who had both taken a seat on the wobbly chairs.

"He'll be here, Boss," Desmond bolstered, "We're early. He'll be here soon." The small rowing boats swayed gently at their moorings and the water swished. It was peaceful, yet both men had been worried about Al's temper, noticing him flop firmly onto the chair.

"Jeez, man. You wanna fall into the water or somethin'?" Benny sniggered; his laughing quickly being silenced by Desmond's raising hand.

Nearly fifteen tedious minutes had painfully passed. Still, the men stayed; Benny inspected the fish in the lake's clear water, Desmond surveyed the mountains, and Al buried his face in the sunlight.

"Fuck it, let's go," Al grumbled and lifted himself using the chair's armrests.

"Wait, Boss, give Mister Galvani a chance," said Desmond.

"How long does he want us to wait?" Al retorted after halting in his tracks.

Benny turned around and claimed, "If you think about it, a train ain't gonna need robbin' if the meetin' never took place."

To their surprise, *someone* did arrive, treading their heels onto the hard sand and verging toward the dry dock with a folder pressed under his thin arm. "The Lost Doggies," the quaint, young newcomer guffawed, tightly shaking Benny's hand. "It's a beautiful view, ain't it?"

"Truly," said Benny after not freeing his hand. "Wait a second, kid," he eyed his young face, "I know you ain't Galvani."

Forcing his hand away from Benny's harsh clutch, he snarled, "Yeah, I'm not Lloyd. I'm his son. The name's Lynch."

THOSE LUCKY FELLAS: PART 1

Al settled beside Desmond, who met the aberrant man, and he, too, plopped onto a white chair and threw the folder onto his lap. Faintly, Al sighed, but Lynch caught sight of him. "Mister King, cheer up, buddy," he said and tapped his knuckle onto Al's knee.

"Where is your father?" Al immediately thrusted, gruffly.

With a blank face, Lynch looked at Al and said, "He's in a meeting. That's why *I'm* here."

"A *meeting*?" questioned Al, facing Benny and Desmond before eyeballing Lynch, again, "What meeting? He should be here. Your old man should be *here*. I ain't settlin'—"

"It is what it is," Lynch disrupted, sharply.

Those remarks caused Al to straighten his back and adjust his deep red tie. "This attitude of yours... it won't play well, boy," he hissed at Lynch, "so you'd best speak in your head first before you open your mouth at me. Ya understand?"

Lynch nodded.

"And why are you so damn late?" Al growled like a wolf.

"What?" Lynch had addressed.

"It's just a simple question," said Al, breaking into silence, but he repeated himself once more; very slowly this time. "*Why* are you so goddamn *late*?"

"Look," said Lynch, jerking upright in his chair, "I don't want any trouble. I'm sorry for—"

"For bein' late?" Al hampered. "Or are you sorry for your lack of respect? *Or* your shortage of manners?"

Tranquility returned, as they all refused to talk, but it was a meeting, nonetheless.

"We're here," said Desmond, putting his hands out to stop the quarrelling, "Let's just have the meeting and go home."

Benny was too amused and stayed mute, tapping his toes onto the wooden planks beneath him.

"Gentlemen, I'm filling in for my father. Everything he wants ya'll to know is in here," said Lynch, holding the folder above his head and twitching it in the air, then commending it to Desmond.

"See? It isn't difficult being polite, is it, son?" Desmond stated, gripping onto the heavy folder. "It's quite heavy," he said, staring at Lynch.

"Yeah... so?"

"It don't need to be. We're *robbing* a train, not *building* one," Desmond flung back.

Lynch pointed his thin finger at the chunky folder and said, "All the information you'll need is in *that* folder. What type of train it is, what you'll be stealing and its route, *including* stations. My old man did some planning beforehand, as you can pro'ly tell."

Shortly after, feet stomped across the wooden dock and caught the attention of the group, as the thumping grew louder. A somewhat middle-aged man, dressed in a dark green and light brown suit, breathed heavily, lounging a hand on his waist and was accompanied by another mature man.

"Didn't think your ass would make it here today, Lloyd," Al expressed.

"Yeah, well, I'm here," Lloyd panted. "Sorry, gentlemen, I had to run a while."

"And we had to wait for a *long* time, Mister Galvani," said Al, scowling.

Lloyd promptly tapped on his son's shoulder and flicked his finger up. "I told you to explain what's in the folder, not just hand it over, idiot!"

"Sorry, Pa," Lynch spoke in a hushed tone.

"And you expect me to hand everything over to you? Go home. Now!" he gnarled.

And with that, Lynch abandoned the docks and scuffed toward the sidewalk. He did not look back and instead dug his head in shame. Pulling in the chair closer to the group, Lloyd took a seat and the man with him was deathly quiet. Probably a bodyguard, Benny thought.

"Mister Galvani, your son is a fool," Al said, sternly, looking at Lloyd directly.

"He ain't just a *fool*," Benny included. "He's a *moron*."

Lloyd grinned and said, "Sadly... I agree," then stuck out his hand toward Desmond. "Hand over the folder and I'll explain the job. *Properly*."

Desmond delivered the thick folder into Lloyd's creased hand and uttered, "Here you go."

Undeterred by the chilling breeze, Lloyd prolonged his digging through the folder, as if he was acting like this purposefully, but the men watched and bit their tongues.

"Take your time, friend," stifled Benny, cleaning his glasses with a clean cloth and sitting them gently on his face.

Al cracked his knuckles. "Why'd ya set a meetin' out here?" he said, scrutinizing Lloyd.

"It's a happy little town!" said Mister Galvani, chirpily. "I thought it might cheer you miserable folk up."

Al forced his finger down, pointing at the floor. "No, I meant... Why *here*? This ain't the ideal weather to be sittin' by a lake."

A deep sigh sprung from Lloyd and his face was expressionless when he said, "It's a beautiful weather, Mister King, so that's why."

Seething in silence, Al ogled Lloyd. "That *meeting* of yours... you had a week spare. You should've been *here* earlier. And your son was late, too. Does that run in the family?"

"Gentlemen!" Desmond intruded. "Shall we get to business?"

Al's eye was fixed on Lloyd's pale face. "Right," Al said bluntly, and saw the man scour through the folder once more.

Most of its contents looked like gibberish, Al pondered.

He was right.

"Let's get back down to business, Mister Galvani," Desmond asserted. "We only need the main rundown. Nothing fancy and certainly nothing unrelated, if you don't mind."

"If you say so," Lloyd subdued.

He removed a few creased papers and presented them to Al and Desmond. Benny leaned closer to see the papers, but had no luck, and watched the glinting water of the vast lake instead.

"Crates?" asked Desmond, who inspected the papers.

They revealed grayish pictures of wooden crates of different sizes; small, large and one that was too immense to be lifted by one man.

"*Exactly*. They're *special*," said Lloyd, handing one more picture to Benny.

"What color are the crates?" Benny asked, waving the paper toward Lloyd.

"The color doesn't matter. If it has a white star painted on, I *want* it," Lloyd spoke like he was drooling.

"What's in 'em?" Al raised, shifting his eyes from the pictures to Lloyd.

"That I cannot say," he hurled back and spoke hastily.

Peeved, Desmond edged himself forward. "Mister Galvani, we *need* to know what we're takin' from that train."

"Weapons. That's all," he said, but his grin felt like a mimic as Desmond quickly discerned.

"I'm hiring you because I know you gentlemen will get the job done. Matter of fact, you're the only ones that can." Straight away, his finger probed at the picture held by Benny. "You see those white stars?" Lloyd announced. "Those are the crates I want. Everything else is yours. I don't care what you do, just get me those crates. Six in total. I counted."

The papers crinkled in the breeze. Meanwhile, Desmond scanned the pictures, trying to find anything odd.

"Who took these?" he asked.

In no hurry, the folder was handed over to the bodyguard, still riveted beside Lloyd. "In all honesty, I did."

Al was confused and asked, "Why not take the crates right then?"

He adjusted his eyepatch and sat up, resting the paper onto his shaking legs.

"I can't just *grab* them, Mister King," said Lloyd, reaching down into the folder. "But... I *did* manage to find out the train's route. Don't worry," he stuck in and pointed at his drawing, "the train travels all over Crown Summit with each complete journey taking, *roughly*, about two hours... Including stops. It *is* a freight train, after all."

Probingly, Desmond spoke loudly, "You got an idea of *when* and *where* the crates will offload or how we'll be boarding the train?"

"Crates'll be on the train at the main station by five tomorrow evening, which means you've got twenty minutes to grab those crates and drag your asses back *before* it reaches the next stop. That's all I know. If I knew *where* they were going, I would've done the job myself," Lloyd spat at the group. "So, once they've been unloaded, we've lost them. Do not let that happen!"

"And how are we boardin' the damn thing?" Benny suggested, flicking his wrist.

"Explosives."

Worried, the men stared at one another despite Lloyd displaying an eerie grin.

"You've gone mad. We don't blow up trains," said Benny.

"No, you'll be blowing up the *track*," Lloyd replied, breathing heavily. "Or... I don't know... You want to *walk* onto the train?" he began to laugh.

"*Tomorrow* is too soon, don't you think? And I reckon you'll supply these *explosives*, correct?" Desmond enquired, looking over at Al.

"I figured you might say that," Lloyd replied. "I've done *most* of the planning for you, and a guy of mine will deliver the explosives tomorrow to your *fancy* house. Nothing fancy, just sticks of dynamite." He pointed at the folder again, giving it a little wave. "Everything you need to know is in *here*."

Benny turned to Lloyd. "Listen, Mister Galvani, enough talkin'. Just tell us... Where do we meet after this blows over?"

Lloyd sneered. "As soon as you get the job done, meet me at the very north of Crown Summit. There's an old cliffside there; a beautiful place."

"Yeah, I know that place," Benny affirmed.

Lloyd grabbed the folder and turned toward Benny. "Take

this, Mister Falcon," he said, passing it discreetly to him. "I've already told you *and* given you everything you'll need. I don't care how you do this, just deliver me them damn crates!"

Benny stuck up his finger. "How much are you payin' us?" he wedged in.

The silence was shattered when Lloyd let out a deep breath. "Five thousand dollars."

"Ten," Benny grunted, peeping over his spectacles with his head tilted downward.

"*Five*," Lloyd snapped back.

"*Ten,*" riposted Al, clearing his throat. He pointed a finger at the man and jerked his wrist vertically. "You want those crates, and we *want* ten thousand dollars," he said and flaunted a smirk. "Do we have an agreement?"

To Galvani, Al's sternness was palpable that he was compelled to agree and for that reason, they firmly shook hands, but neither of them smiled.

"We have an agreement," Lloyd confirmed, letting go of Al's powerful hand and resting against the stiff plastic chair. "But if you fail me... Let's just hope you *don't* fail me. For both our sakes."

"We shall see, Mister Galvani. We shall see," Al made clear.

Chapter Sixteen

Lonesome Roads

When the meeting had drawn to a close, they stood and walked across the dock, tramping against the wet wood and exchanging very few words. Benny glared at his lambent pocket watch and had noticed that far too much time had slipped by.

He displayed the face to Desmond and whispered, "Far too much bickering by those clowns," before slipping it back into his pocket.

Desmond chuckled and remarked, "What can I say, Benny?"

They continued strolling along with the rest as they landed on the icy sidewalk and listened to it crumble under their feet. Idle cars were aligned across the sides of the main street; their colors reflecting in the sprightly sunlight. The people of Silver Springs seemed merry, greeting one another and the men, too!

"Fellas, I will see you tomorrow," said Galvani, turning around to face the gang. "Do not disappoint me."

Al and Lloyd firmly exchanged a handshake right when a group of stylish men from across the street caught their first glimpse; maybe three or four ambling along the sidewalk.

"Just ignore 'em, Galvani," hissed Benny, stepping closer toward him and gripping on his shoulder. "Don't do anythin' hasty."

Eagerly, Desmond stepped back and headed for his car; Al tagging along, waving his hand at Lloyd. "Come on, Benny," said Al, turning his head to see over his shoulder.

"Peacekeepers," Lloyd whispered.

THOSE LUCKY FELLAS: PART 1

"Can't be. They ain't comin' all the way out to Silver Springs," Benny subdued, urging Lloyd to pay attention to him by lugging his stiff shoulder.

"They have now and they're probably here for *us*," said his bodyguard, hunching behind a parked car and removing his pistol from inside his jacket.

In no time, Desmond froze and Al swirled, inching his hand forward, hushing, "Mister Galvani, calm down."

The men dressed in gray and blue halted and leered at the rest.

"Hit the deck!" crowed Lloyd as he and his accomplice opened fire.

Empty shell casings clattered against the sidewalk and the screams from the people of the small town were muted by the ear-splitting sound of the guns firing.

"What the hell are ya doin'?" Benny exclaimed, ducking behind a car and jerking his pistol into his hand.

He was joined by Al and Desmond, as they all returned fire, leaning over the parked vehicles and ducking again.

Benny shot an officer on the side of his hip, and he toppled onto his back, grunting. But when he turned his head toward Lloyd, his accomplice had been shot, too.

A hail of bullets flew by, piercing the doors and windows of cars and some striking stores, mailboxes and trees. The birds darted from the trees and had rushed over the lake.

"Get your asses outta here!" Lloyd screamed, peering over his cover and shooting.

"Let's go!" Al roared, taking the lead and creeping around the corner of a small building.

"We're leaving Galvani?" questioned Desmond, rushing

along and tailing Al with his head tucked.

"You heard the man!" Benny yelled and followed. "This ain't our fight!"

They rushed toward the car, brushing the panicking towns-folk aside, and hopped in, slamming the doors shut. The drumming from the engine could be felt, but the ringing from their ears silenced its sound.

Al was slouched in his seat and peeked out of the window. "Take us home!" he shouted and slammed his hand onto the folder next to him.

"Where do ya think he's takin' us?" Benny responded, who was rocking around in the back just as Desmond reversed onto the slippery road.

"That was close. Pretty convenient for them to show up *after* the meeting," Desmond brought up.

Only a few minutes had passed by until they reached the smooth roads out of Silver Springs and, without wanting to draw any more attention, they steadily drove along its smooth surface, overwhelmed by the outstanding scenery.

Exhausted, Benny watched as Al open his mouth and say something to Desmond, but he was not listening. His mind was too focused on the job ahead—it had been too long since the gang had been involved with such a task, yet Benny believed they could still pull it off.

The snow winked at him when it caught the sunlight and he closed his eyes and leaned against the seat, slowly falling asleep.

Finally, the bumpy roads came forth, waking up the old man.

"Jeez," said Benny when a wheel clipped a large rock.

THOSE LUCKY FELLAS: PART 1

"We're almost home, boys," Al declared; his hand had remained inside the folder.

"Yeah, I could tell," Benny mumbled, bent his back and rested his head in his hands. He stared at the fluffy carpet underneath him and closed his eyes just as the car rocked over the broken dirt roads.

"We best not tell the rest about what Galvani did, ya understand?" Al said, sharply, watching the other two closely. Benny put his thumb up lazily, and Desmond bowed his head and was still concentrating on creeping over the bumps.

Home was in sight after they traversed over the final few bumps on the road and Benny was never this excited to return to his bedroom. "Finally, I can put my head to rest. It's killin' me."

"Oh, we still got the whole job to discuss with the rest of the fellas before you can go to bed," said Desmond, parking near the grand fountain.

"Good call, Mister Kane," said Al, hurrying out of his seat.

Sluggishly, Benny left, too, and grunted when approaching the front doors of the manor. "Best make it quick."

Once inside, it was calm and silent, at least in the hallway. The children were delightedly playing with their toys or watching television in the cozy living room, as Benny could see flashes of various colors splattering against the walls.

"Hey, honey, where are the men?" asked Al, cradling his wife and kissing her cheek.

She giggled and replied, "Last I saw them, they were in the backyard," and let go of her husband after greeting the other two.

"Let's go," Mister King said to his men and turned to Caroline again. "We'll be havin' another meetin' tonight, honey," he stated, smiling at her and wondered down the wide and pretty hallway. Benny and Desmond followed; hearing Al call out to the rest. Once they had gathered, Al said, lowering his tone, "Gentlemen, we got a meetin' tonight. 'Bout the train job. Keep it between us... For now."

Papers were scattered across the wide table; drawings, notes, and even scrunched up paper balls rolled around the wooden floor. A map was pinned across the long wall, with Desmond pointing at certain crosses and circles that he had marked.

It was late into the night. Drained bottles and empty glasses were plumped onto the table beside the men and the scent of whiskey made the air feel thick and sticky.

"The train'll stop when we blow up the tracks," Carson explained to Reese, who began to wipe his oily nose.

"Why don't we just sneak onto the train when it's stationed? Wouldn't it be less obvious?" Reese replied, whilst resting his chin onto his palm.

"Far too many people are gon' be at the station," said Houston. "So, if we sneak on, there's a slim chance we'll be gettin' off quietly at the next station. Can't really be drawin' attention, can we?"

Carson glanced at the map, curiously. "The tracks would be blown up *before* that train arrives at the second station, correct?"

"Yes. Hopefully it stops, too," Desmond confirmed.

Al stood against the shut window and observed the room. "We're blowin' it up because it's *faster*. Nobody's gonna be hearin' it in the mountains."

THOSE LUCKY FELLAS: PART 1

Houston perched on his chair after stretching his legs. "So, the train's gone off the rails. Then we just take the crates with white stars painted on 'em?"

"Exactly," Desmond said, slowly. "I don't see why that's so difficult to understand."

"It's Reese, he's bein' clueless, like always," Carson laughed.

"Hey, white stars on crates... Ain't that military?" Houston wondered, pointing his hand into the air.

Carson played around with his empty whiskey glass and plotted it onto the table beside him. "Probably, but why would it be on a regular freight train?"

"Fellas, listen," said Benny, arching his back and listening to it crackle, "Tomorrow is important... to Al, at least. Let's just pay attention and get this meetin' over with."

With heavy steps, Al approached the table and dumped his hands against its polished surface. "No... Not just to *me*," he retaliated. "We're doing this for *all of us*!" His eye was fixed on Benny, before intensely glaring at the rest. "This job is... Look, we owe Mister Galvani a favor. Ain't no steppin' back, 'specially not from a man like him."

Benny shrugged.

"Back to it," Desmond exhaled and turned to the map once more. "Here, we'll arrive tomorrow at five... *sharp*. We blow up the tracks and wait for the train."

His finger ran across the enormous black and white map.

"Then we wait?" Reese buzzed, elbows on the table.

"Bingo!" said Carson, "You got that part right. Train should only take a couple of minutes to reach us, right?" he pressed after looking over to Desmond.

"That's right," he said back.

"Even if the train don't stop, it'll fall over. We're stealin' from it all the same," Houston put forth and drew his eyes over to the map.

To pass the time, Benny skimmed over the label of an empty whiskey bottle. By now, they had already reviewed their plan countless times. "Once we rob the train, gettin' the crates off and all, we make a run for it, go straight to His Majesty, Mister Galvani. Poor fella must be bored hangin' around the cliffside."

"Take this seriously, Benny," Al huffed. "If you recall, we only kill those who're gonna be a problem."

Carson sat up, leaned over to Benny and said, "Mister Falcon, your Hudson Hornet will be ready tomorrow. You takin' it to the job?"

"Of course!" Benny smiled, as he was pleased to hear those words. "And thank you, Mister Montgomery!"

Al, who was still light on his toes and overlooking the table, flicked his hand and mentioned, "I presume we're all on the same page, surely, and we can conclude this meetin' of ours."

Several hours had elapsed and the immutable arguing and babbling had finally ceased. Each of them comprehended their roles, and they were all set. The long-awaited day was approaching and something truly unforgettable lay on the horizon.

Chapter Seventeen

Caesar

A continuous dinging sound had echoed through the empty hallway moments after the sun had emerged, splashing the great halls of the manor with bursts of orange and yellow. It was much too early for someone to be calling, thought Benny, lifting the copper brown telephone and hushing the racket.

"Good morning," said the crooked voice, pausing between words. "May I speak with Mister Falcon?"

"Speakin'," Benny said, like he was whispering.

"Ah, good! How are you doing, my boy?"

"I didn't sleep well, if I'm bein' honest," Benny patted his eyelid and from under his glasses.

"I do apologize for calling so early, Benny, but there is something we need to discuss. Thought I should grab you first thing in the morning," said the raspy voice.

Benny stared blankly out of the window, which looked like an orange canvas and his mind came back to him. "Hold on... Caesar?"

The gruff voice laughed, "You're goddamn right!"

"Jeez, I didn't think you'd still be breathin'!"

"It's been way too long, Mister Falcon. I wish to have called you for a different matter, but... you can't have everything in life, I suppose."

"Somethin' wrong?" Benny needled and his voice had gotten deeper.

"For you fellas? Probably. Listen, Benny, come meet me at my place. You still remember where I live, don't you?"

Benny chuckled. "Still livin' in that tiny shack?"

"So, you do remember? I'll be here all day, so drop by before your *job*," Caesar said, as his voice began to fade.

"How d'ya find *that* out?" Benny countered, bewildered.

"I know many things. Be seeing you shortly, Mister Falcon."

The call had ended and the echo from the beeping had lingered in his ear, which grew faint when the tired man returned the telephone to its hook, bumping and clicking the plastic. He yawned and descended the white stairs; the last few lit by the golden sunrise, and took to the cold kitchen.

Upon his arrival, Benny, without haste, opened a cupboard door, trying his best to not let it squeak, and reached out for two boxes of cereal. "Cheerios or Rice Krispies?" he mumbled to himself until he settled with waffles. Once the silver toaster had chimed, the waffles were placed onto a blue dinner plate. Maple syrup poured onto the stack of crispy, yellow waffles, and the sweet aroma filled his nose as he dug in.

Delicate footsteps converged toward the calm kitchen; too quiet to be heard by Benny, and he was startled when his eyes brushed over Sloane.

"Good morning, Mister Falcon," she said, attiring dark red, silky pajamas and fluffy black shoes.

"Jeez, woman," he cried and coughed when the syrup stuck against his throat. "Mornin."

Sloane laughed and covered her mouth with her hand. "I am so sorry, Benny," she responded with a heartier laugh.

"Oh, you think that's funny?" Benny chuckled and faced the pretty figure.

"Why are *you* awake so early? This isn't like you, Benny. Of all the people here, *you* get up last." After turning the handle of the kitchen sink, Sloane let it pour for a few seconds before filling a mug with the cold water.

"I couldn't sleep. Matter of fact, I *hardly* slept," he said, sawing a knife into the waffle's golden crust.

Sloane headed toward the fridge after rinsing her mug and leaving it out to dry by the sink. She unlatched the bulky fridge door and removed a carton of fresh orange juice and placed it beside Benny.

"Thank you," he said, softly.

"Tell me, Benny," said Sloane, determined to find answers from him. "You going somewhere? What are you doing?" Concernedly, she sat on a stool beside him and placed her warm hand on his. "Mister Falcon, you can tell me *anything*. You seem a little... distressed," her heavenly voice called out.

Benny chortled. "I ain't distressed. It's *you people* I'm worried about."

"How so?" she said, her eyes widened.

He turned and peered into her shining eyes and saw nothing but her innocence stare back. "I'm meetin' an old friend of mine. That's why I'm awake this early. And... we've got a job this evenin'."

Sloane's pretty face contorted with displeasure, and her jaw became tense. "A job?"

"For one of your grandfather's friends," Benny said and ate the last piece of his waffles and played with the remaining drops of maple syrup with his fork.

"But *why*?" her words hurled toward the old man. "*We* do not *need* any more money. This family—all of us—have more than enough to keep us going."

"It's not about money, anymore, Sloane" Benny said bitterly. "We do this to keep you all safe. To make a future, where you can wake up and smell the flowers we've left behind."

"I thought my grandfather left everything behind. He promised the world will become safer for us now that you all quit," Sloane stated, as her voice became quiet.

"I understand, Sloane, but we've gotta tie loose ends or there won't be a safer world for any of us. We keep gettin' dragged back into it," Benny lifted himself from the stool, twisted the cap of the orange juice carton and poured it into a glass. "Your grandfather... Al is a *strange* one. Don't let it run in the family," he added, smiling at Sloane and gulping the flavorsome juice. The empty, stained dinner plate was removed from the table and Benny settled them by the sink.

"Leave them. Let me wash up," Sloane said, rising from the stool and letting the water flow.

Benny patted her shoulder, breezily, and took to the kitchen door. "I won't be long. You're in charge around here, so be sure to keep everyone in check."

Sloane tittered.

A sharp knock on the front door startled Sloane, but Benny reached for the iron handles. They never had a visitor this early. The cold breeze had swept into the hallway once the doors were ajar and before Benny stood a man donning a blue checkered shirt and brown pants; blackened patches on both, and his blue cap.

"Mornin', mister," he said, showing his teeth through his grin.

"What do you want?"

He handed a shiny key to Benny.

THOSE LUCKY FELLAS: PART 1

"Your Hudson Hornet, sir. Or whoever it belongs to."

"Ah, right," Benny mumbled and let the mechanic drop the key into his palm. "Carson paid you, has he not?"

The mechanic nodded.

"Sure has!" he said joyfully, and tipped his hat to Benny, who tilted his head in return.

"Thank you, I appreciate that. Perfect timin', too!" Benny acknowledged and shook the man's hand, bidding him a farewell soon after.

He lit a cigar and savored its vanilla flavor, and glared at his pristine Hudson Hornet like the first time he had bought it; enamored by its deep black paint and chrome bumpers.

Tardy heels clicked behind him. Otis had tromped from the manor's great hallway and into the front yard.

"Otis," Benny greeted him.

"That's the first time you ain't said anythin' bad. It's like you're *happy* to see me," said Otis, yawning loudly.

"What're ya doin' awake this early?" Benny asked, watching the old coot settle on the bench.

"Thought I'd say goodbye before I left," he announced and scratched his back with his good arm.

"You're leavin' this early?"

Nodding, Otis shrugged.

"I know about this job you fellas are doin' later tonight. I ain't stupid. I want out before you get back and I thought *now* would be a... good time, you know."

Benny laughed and said, "You weren't stayin' long, anyway, but it was good havin' ya, I suppose."

Otis stood and stepped toward Benny, tightly wrapping him with his right arm.

"I'm gon' miss ya, boy. Wherever you're goin' *now*, I ain't gonna be here when you get back. So... this is farewell."

Although Benny forced himself to return a hug, he felt relieved.

"Goodbye, Otis. Don't go gettin' shot in your other arm, you hear?"

Before too long, Benny cruised over the nearby bloated hills and broke off from the main road onto a dirty path. He drove deeper into a wondrous forest, where the trees began to grow taller and thicker, forming a canopy overhead that bunged most of the warm sunlight.

A cramped, but well-formed hut was in sight, impelling Benny to park by its side and avoid scaring the charming horses. A forty-eight-star flag hung above the front door.

Taking a deep breath, he shut off the engine and stepped out of the car. The metal latch clicked, and he strolled over the dead grass until he spotted a figure resting on a tree log by a small campfire; an elderly man with his back turned to him.

"Hello, Caesar," said Benny patiently, hopping over the large log.

The enfeebled elderly man clung to his walking stick, but Benny flicked his hand, urging him to stay seated and squatted down with him.

"Twen'y years since I last saw you, my boy," Caesar's withered voice called out, patting Benny's hand. "Time... Time went by *real fast*."

"It has," said Benny, lightly.

Caesar, with his wizened smile, turned and said, "How've you been keeping?"

Benny exhaled deeply, as though he was tired.

THOSE LUCKY FELLAS: PART 1

"What can I say? I suppose it's been all right. Just... keepin' busy."

Caesar played around with the logs under the fire, poking them with a stick.

"You retired and came back. That's... unheard of." He placed the stick against his leg and perked up, then pivoted to Benny again. "You know, most people run away from a life like yours."

"Yeah, well, you can't always *run*," said Benny, listening to the fire crackle.

Caesar stood and relied upon his walking stick, shepherding Benny to his two horses; one dark brown and the other black.

"The horses need to walk, Mister Falcon. I don't like them standing in one place."

"You sure you can still ride?" Benny chuckled and stroked the side of the majestic black horse. It felt like velvet, he thought.

"Sometimes, you've got to give up your car and settle with an old horse," Caesar smiled and despite his crookedness, he climbed onto the saddle with ease.

"If you say so," said Benny and lifted himself onto the saddle, too, patting the horse's elongated neck.

With a gentle tug of the leather reins, Caesar rode onto a path leading into the forest and Benny galloped behind him.

"Don't fall behind, Benny."

Dourly, the two men rode with the sound of the hoofs muffled by the carpet of dead leaves and soggy ground. Trees towered on both sides of the path, forging wooden walls and the air was fresh, scented with the earthy aroma of mud and moss.

"This is pretty peaceful," said Benny, swaying with his horse.

"See, my boy? Learn to live a little," Caesar added, combing the brown mane with his fingers.

They grew quiet as they traveled deeper, allowing the blissful surroundings to envelop them in an arcadian tranquility. Leaves rustled and birds called, and the balmy breeze weaved the branches.

Caesar halted and turned on his horse. "Hey, I want to show you something," he said. "Kick her a little, she'll follow me."

Pivoting back around, his horse cantered, thudding along the dirt, and just like Caesar said, Benny's horse followed. Eventually, they had reached a straight, even path and Caesar was looking for some excitement.

"Benny! Run with me!" he cheered, and his horse galloped, rapidly thumping the ground.

"I'm right behind ya!" Benny chanted and the black horse sprinted through the forest; its fabulous mane fluttering in the wind and its head nodding as it galloped.

They neared the edge of the forest, where the ground became rocky and they began to waver up a slope, ascending above the enormous trees and brushing against the clouds.

"Steady on, old girl," Caesar muttered, patting the animal's neck. He turned his head over his shoulder and said, "Careful, Benny. Stay calm and she will, too."

Benny nodded, petted the eager horse and said out loud, "That's a good girl," and his hand began to rub on her neck.

Upon climbing to the mountain's peak, the two reined

their horses and glared at the incredible view below. Across the glorious valleys and hills, trees were dotted alongside country roads, mountains slumbered, and the roads were unbound.

"Jeez, I haven't since Knox this pretty in *years*!" Benny exclaimed.

"Out here, you can fly as high as you wish. Take a few steps back and just let it *all* in," said Caesar cheerfully.

"Knox truly is somethin' else," said Benny, as he breathed in the crisp air.

Caesar observed Benny. "Let me explain something to you, Mister Falcon," he said, and Benny's eyes clocked him.

"What's that?" he asked, hopping off the saddle and holding onto the reins and overlooking the forest.

"Regret is a shadow that follows us through life; a reminder of the paths not taken and the choices we left behind. The more you choose to feed it, the more desperate you will become."

Benny inhaled and said, "I don't really regret much, Caesar."

"We all see it in the end," Caesar clicked his fingers and grinned. "You'll see when you get to my age. Some have bigger shadows than others."

"Livin' alone really *does* make a man lose his mind," Benny chuckled, and Caesar laughed, too.

They returned to the hut, Benny tied the horses, and joined the patriarch by the fire.

Harshly, Caesar coughed into his fist and his throat growled, "Forgive me, Benny."

"For what?"

In the stillness, birds sung, and the breeze swept through the branches, causing the trees to wave.

"I brought you into this gang. All those years ago. When you were just a kid," said Caesar; his voice cracked and trembled when he spoke.

"The gang is all I had when my mother died. Matter of fact, I should be thankin' you, Caesar, for givin' me a chance," Benny responded and placed his hand onto the Caesar's thin shoulder.

A light-hearted laugh broke from him. "Forty-six years ago, I started the gang, and it looks like you bastards are still kicking. We've... *You've* all come a long way." With his curved back, Caesar reached for the iron kettle that hung over the campfire, but Benny was fast enough to beat him to it.

"I've got it," mumbled Benny, tightly grabbing its thick handle.

"Thank you. Pour some for yourself while you're at it," Caesar insisted, pointing at two overturned iron mugs.

"What is it?" asked Benny, tilting the kettle and pouring the sizzling liquid into the mugs.

"Tea," Caesar responded. He grabbed the first mug from Benny and bobbed his head before blowing into it. The steam rose from the mug and mixed with the fresh morning air; all the while, Caesar shrouded the mug with his numb hands. Benny poured the flower-scented tea into his mug, too, and found himself relaxing next to the old man again after returning the kettle to the fire.

"Smells good," Benny said, breathing heavily.

Caesar cackled and said, "A twelve-year-old disobedient Benny Falcon joins The Lost Dogs and I had to convince Al you'll bring good stuff to the table. And now look at you... almost in your sixties." His lips smacked one another after he took another sip, trying to savor the sweet taste.

"It didn't take much to convince him, did it?"

"No," Caesar claimed and slurped onto the tea; a little louder this time, and casually turned to ponder at the remarkable Hudson Hornet.

The fragrant tea heated Benny's throat and he found himself feeling mellow.

"I understand you've retired and decided to settle on a quieter life, wantin' nothin' of the gang no more," he spoke, mildly, "But... Why'd ya call?"

His drowsy eyes shut. "I want to ask for a favor. It's ain't a *personal* favor, because it'll help you boys out more than me."

"What's that?" Benny became curious and drummed his thumb on the tip of his mug.

With a deep breath, Caesar sighed and opened his eyes, glaring at the small fire.

"This train you're robbin' later tonight. Mister Lloyd Galvani put you up to it?"

He felt his heart flutter in an instant and his eyes widened.

"Actually, it was Mister King, but Lloyd swayed him. Havin' said that, you took a good guess. You mind explainin'?"

"I have eyes and ears everywhere, Mister Falcon," Caesar asserted, then stared at Benny's pale face.

"What of Galvani?" Benny asked, astonished by the old man's nimble thinking.

The fire rustled, and the wind spoke through the trees, creating hurls of faint whispers around them.

"I want Lloyd and his people dead," said Caesar, crankily, scowling and narrowing his eyes at Benny, who was taken by surprise.

"From one job to another. You're serious, ain't ya?" said

Benny and his voice hollowed out.

His tea swiveled around in the mug, gathering the tiny pieces of tea leaves.

An itch on Caesar's neck had caused a drop of tea to land onto his sleeve, and he played around with the stain left behind.

"These *weapons* he wants from the train aren't ordinary weapons," he specified. "Lloyd knows what's in 'em, of course, but that son of a bitch is planning something *big*."

Gradually, Benny lost interest in his tea—whiskey would have been a better choice, he thought, but he did not want to upset Caesar.

"I ain't quite gettin' where you're goin' with this, if I'm honest."

Caesar looked at Benny and shook his head.

"They're *explosives*," he said. "Heavy machine guns, too. It don't take a genius to know what you can do with *all that* firepower. A man who stops caring is a dangerous man."

"Goddamnit," Benny whispered.

"What else didn't he tell you?" Caesar raised. "I bet he said he doesn't know where the crates are going, did he not?" Caesar's anger was apparent at the mention of Lloyd's name.

"Yeah, all he said was... *weapons*," said Benny.

Caesar still glanced at Benny and mentioned, "You didn't think of questioning that? He's a sneaky cocksucker."

With deliberate care, he lowered the mug to the ground, avoiding any further spills, twisted his shaking body, and stared at Benny.

"Listen, man, do not allow Lloyd to get his hands on those crates," he spat his words and his eyes filled with hatred. "All you gotta do is rob the train, and I don't care how you do this, but I want the Galvani family out of the picture. I want *my* gang safe and *you* want to retire. Only way is to shed old skin."

Nodding gradually, Benny placed his hand onto Caesar's.

"You have my word," he said. "But first, I gotta know somethin'."

Caesar raised an eyebrow and respectfully asked, "What is it, my boy?"

A smile broke out from Benny. "*Caesar* ain't your real name."

Caesar beamed a smile back and shook his head, brushing his very few white hairs through his fingers.

"What are you getting at, Benny?"

"So, what is it?" he remarked, with his smile still glued to his face.

"Don't push it, Benny," Caesar returned and turned toward the now dying fire. Grasping the end of his walking stick, he rose to his feet, listening to his bones crunch, but Benny had held onto his back and arm before he could try himself.

"I'll do it," Benny expressed, leaning into Caesar and wrapping his arms around him, to which he returned the hug, too.

"You ain't going to need to convince Al about taking down Lloyd," said Caesar.

"I gotta think of somethin' to say to him," Benny stated, letting go and stood parallel to the bony man.

"You ain't going to need to convince him," he repeated, grinning this time. "Al will see it for himself when the time comes. He'll *have* a plan."

"All right," Benny chuffed and nodded at the short old man and heaved toward his Hudson Hornet.

Chapter Eighteen

Breaking the Train

It was almost time. Their eagerness grew as the hour drew near. Benny kneeled by a tombstone. His eyes felt moist, but he did not shed a tear when he stared at the marble and its chiseled inscription; *In Loving Memory of Katherine Falcon, 1869-1904.*

"Here you go, Mother. In case I don't get a chance later," he whispered in a soft tone, burying a few bonny snowdrops at the foot of the stone. "I know lilies were your favorite, but we're gon' have to wait for the summer to get those."

Benny kissed his right index and middle fingers and held it against the tombstone, then walked down a pebbled path, carefully wandering through a hill, where his Hudson Hornet had waited at the bottom.

On the homeward journey, the roads were hushed, and the radio had ceased, and Benny enjoyed the serenity of the early afternoon sky, piping birds and the crispy wind blowing against his arm and head. His peace of mind had been shattered when he arrived at the front yard of the great manor.

"Move your ass!" yelled Houston, stabbing his finger at Reese.

"Looks like we're gonna be tardy, boys!" Carson shouted, lifting a wooden box into the trunk of his black 1949 Mercury Eight.

"We'll make it. Do not worry," Desmond reassured the rest.

Benny halted by the gate and left his car, marching over to the busy crowd, who carried small, illuminated lanterns. "Everyone ready?" he asked, adjusting his black leather gloves and the sleeves of his long black coat.

"Pretty much," replied Houston, nodding his head. "Just waitin' on *you*, Boss."

Benny saw the men carry their firearms; rifles and submachine guns mostly and bobbed his head. He cleared his throat and said, "We're gonna get through this, gentlemen. It's a simple job. We've had worse in the past and got through it, so this ain't gon' be a problem."

His growling, deep voice was interrupted by Al, who treaded heavily along the paved path, whilst his face was hidden under a black and brown leather cowboy hat. Benny blinked slowly, and the rest felt bemused, displaying empty gazes.

"That train ain't droppin' the crates by the side of the road for us to grab," Al announced, moving the opening of his coat like parting a set of curtains to reveal two impeccable silver Colt New Service revolvers.

"What the hell are you doin'?" fussed Benny, sticking out an open hand at Al.

"What's it look like?" he hissed. "I'm comin' with ya!"

Laughing, Benny approached his boss and rested his hands on his shoulders. "No. You just get to Mister Galvani when the job's done. That was the plan."

"Stayin' home is gettin' me bored. I gotta stretch, so I'm doin' this job *with* you fellas," he said, pushing Benny's hands right away.

The men stared in disbelief.

"All right. Fine," Benny repined. Arguing with Al was hopeless, like beating a dead horse, he thought. "You takin' the lead on this one? Because if you are, I got somethin' to tell ya."

"And what's that?" Al countered, raising an eyebrow and

his chin.

"You'll hear it soon enough," said Benny, flicking his head toward the parked cars. "Let's go, gentlemen," he said.

With that, Benny marshaled the rest to the vehicles; excitement stung them, but they felt troubled, too, and they had every right to be.

Hurriedly, Benny docked himself behind the wheel of his Hudson Hornet and Al perched beside him. Meanwhile, Reese plopped into the back seat.

"Let's get goin'," Al stated, whilst Benny held up his thumb to Carson, who was accompanied by Houston and Desmond.

The pale manor vanished whilst the two cars cruised through the winding, bumpy roads of the hills and cliffs, and the sky had ceased its burning colors.

Navigating methodically through the turns, Benny lowered his window and sniffed the cold air; a hint of pine struck his nose. The night was quiet, as usual, with the occasional rustling of the leaves from the speedy winds, creating shadows in the path of their headlights.

"Steady on, Benny, we've got time," said Al, patiently, as he watched the glowing crescent moon tail them.

"I want this over and done with just as much as everyone else," he replied and swung his eyes from the mirror to the dingy road.

He found it difficult to shake off the dread and discomfort that settled in his chest, but he drove deeper through the grove of soaring trees, regardless.

Reese unlatched the shiny case cover of his steel pocket watch; not long left until the train leaves the station.

"Might wanna speed up, Mister Falcon," he said, resting his

eyes on his watch.

"Why? Are we gettin' late?" Benny put forth with his head turned and chin over his shoulder.

"No, no. We've got plenty o' time," Reese added, stuffing his pocket watch into his pocket.

Benny squinted and peaked at the road. "Then... Never mind," said Benny, lowering his voice and sighing.

Now, they were in the clear; open, flat roads welcomed their fast driving and the alpine trees had turned into shrubs and saplings by the sides of the road, some rubbing against a worn brick wall, too. The street lights, which were sparsely scattered, flickered and created spots of light that flashed into their eyes.

"Country roads ain't much good when it's dark," said Benny, annoyed.

"Almost arrivin', now. We *should* be there in another ten minutes or so," Al said, quietly, watching the silhouettes of the distant enormous mountains.

"That's *if* Benny drives us there in one piece," Reese sat up and chuckled, then stopped. "Please don't go all crazy on the snow... Like you *always* do, Mister Falcon."

Benny snorted. With his arm stretched up and out of the open window, he flicked his wrist and sent his hand flying forward several times, like cracking a whip, and Carson overtook him, dashing in front.

"Good call," said Al, looking into his mirror to see nothing but a black abyss.

The engine howled, drowning out the squelching snow from under the tires as it scurried along the wet road. Above, white stars lustered and the moon hid behind a flimsy cloud.

"We've passed Silver Springs," said Al, pleasantly surprised by the town's nighttime charm; the roads were lined with pretty, black street lights and polished benches sat by the docks. "This town... Somethin' is *seriously wrong* with it."

"How so?" questioned Reese, looking out of both windows by his sides. "The town looked different last time I was here," he inserted, "but it looks prettier!"

Peering behind him, watching Silver Springs disappear into the darkness, Benny said, "You are right, Mister King. Folk here are *far* too happy," and began combing his mutton chops with his hand. "Nobody can be *that* happy!"

Snow, fresh and shimmering, carpeted the road out of Silver Springs, burying parts of it. Carson gradually braked and Benny did, too, but they held their speed across the slippery asphalt and it was not long until their tires had been swallowed by the heaps of snow.

"Steady on, Benny," said Al, who lifted his head to peek over the Hudson Hornet's chrome bumper. "You're doin' fine. Just hold your speed. Take it easy on that gas," he continued.

Benny's hand fought the steering once the wheels began to slip and become lighter.

"That's interestin'," he said, playfully.

"What is?" Al returned, turning his head.

Catching his breath and gripping the steering wheel tighter, Benny replied, "You lecturin' me about drivin'. That's funny!"

Reese clung onto the seat and laughed with Benny. "He's right. Mister King, you always have been a terrible driver. It's no wonder we don't let you drive."

"That's enough, Reese!" Al yelled, rolling down his window and cooling his face with the nipping, piercing wind.

Ahead, Carson plowed mightily through the snow and had made it easier for Benny to follow the tramped down path. Once Carson had reached the top of the snow-covered hill, he waited for Benny, who halted by his side when arriving.

"Mister Montgomery! Why'd ya stop?" shouted Benny, winding down the glass.

"Take the lead, Boss! I don't know the way from here, in all honesty," Carson announced.

"It's a straight road!" said Benny after pointing at the blanched path to the front.

Houston shook his head and leaned out and added, "That's *exactly* what I told him!"

Benny did not want his brain to be filled with the quarreling from the others, so he powered through the deep snow, blowing it upward like dust and soon Carson had tailed his beaten path.

Shortly, they coursed over the hill and onto a flat, white, silky road—without any slipping from the tires. Benny was relieved.

"Say, Mister Falcon," Al said, scratching his forehead. "What was it you wanted to say?"

"What?" replied Benny, cluelessly.

"Back home, in the yard, you said you had somethin' *important* to tell me. What is it?" Al looked over keenly.

"Oh, about that..." Benny stumbled, "I was gon' ask if you *really* trust Mister Galvani."

Al smirked, and Benny knew it was not a good sign.

"We'll see it to the very end," Al said, clearing his throat and watching the stars.

"You don't know what you're talkin' about," Benny said in response, crunching his eyebrows and his jaw became restless.

"Better be careful where you tread, Mister Falcon," Al replied and stared at the road ahead.

"Do you *or* do you *not* trust Lloyd?" Benny said, louder.

Briskly, Al shot his hand up and curled it into a fist, leaving only his index finger extended.

"No. I don't trust that bastard one bit. I never have," Al hissed.

"Then why are we doing this job to begin with?" Reese asked, edging forward.

"I have a card I want to play. That's why I said we'll be seein' it to the very end. Trust me on this," retorted Al, swaying his words to the two.

In due course, they had reached a large, open field; pine trees stood bordering both sides with short grass hugging their trunks and, in the middle, lay a set of luminescent but blemished tracks.

"We made it. Let's get to work," said Benny, coming to a halt by a large boulder. Carson parked beside him, and the men tightly wrapped red bandanas over their mouths and noses.

"Make it quick, boys, we ain't got time to lose," said Al, hurrying out of the car. "Remember, we ain't using our names."

Burying his feet in the snow, Benny turned and skipped over to the Hudson Hornet's trunk, fishing out his untainted Browning Automatic Rifle before shutting it.

Meanwhile, the rest stood with lanterns in their hands and watched as Carson and Desmond fetched the crate of dynamite before rushing over to the tracks, tugging its thick rope handles.

THOSE LUCKY FELLAS: PART 1

"Steady," said Reese, watching from afar.

"Quit standin' there and give them a hand," said Houston, elbowing him in the back.

"No. I ain't going near that," Reese replied, stepping away from Houston.

"Stay put, we've got this!" Carson shouted as he and Desmond set the crate down on a pile of snow.

With great caution, they opened the lid and carefully removed the chunky sticks of dynamite; its long, thin cord was coiled together, like a spider's web, and they handled it delicately.

"Might wanna hurry it up! Train'll be here any moment," howled Benny, peering over his shoulders.

With Desmond feeding the cord into his hand, Carson placed the explosives on the sturdy, steel train tracks, tiptoeing backward and stowing more between the wooden planks.

"Don't go blowing us up, now, you hear?" Desmond chuckled.

"All done," said Carson, standing straight and lifting his leg away from the tracks.

"Let's get going," said Desmond, aligning the cords and laying a path of wire to the rest.

"All right, good job, fellas," Al panted, rubbing his eye from under his eyepatch.

"Why're *you* out of breath? You didn't do anythin'," said Benny.

"Quiet down and hand me your lighter," Al stated, reaching out to the grumbling man.

Benny sneered, removed his engraved lighter from within his woolly coat, and walked past Al. He bent down, flame in hand, and set the cord alight. It sizzled.

"Hold on," mumbled Houston. "You seeing what I am?" he gasped and pointed at an orange light in the distance.

It was as if the sun had risen, but it had only just set!

"Dear God, what is that?" Al muttered. "Get back, boys!" Al shouted, and they dashed behind a small hill; Benny rushed toward the boulder.

As the burning light grew larger, the flame on the cord had almost reached the dynamite.

"Cover your ears, men, this is 'bout to get messy!" stormed Carson, and they did.

At once, a sudden jolt pushed through them, and their ears rang, and their heads vibrated. The steel rails curled, and tiny, sharp pieces of wood scattered across the snow.

"That ought to do it," said Benny, leaning out from the boulder.

"Jesus," Desmond hushed.

The train had arrived. It was fast. And it was on fire. The front had caught the beaten rail and plummeted into the dirt, almost tipping the train, but the rest of the cars had stayed upright on the rail... Luckily.

"Come on! Haul those crates!" Al yowled, taking out his revolvers and marching toward the wounded train. He bent his knees and climbed onto the locomotive.

"You gentlemen go find those crates. I'll go to the boss, make sure he don't screw this up," said Benny, lifting his rifle over his shoulder.

The rest scrambled, rushing up to the hefty boxcars and prying open the ponderous doors; it took all their strength and once inside; they began inspecting the cargo. A large portion of the first car was stacked with boxes and crates of clothing and furniture—nothing of which interested the men—but they kept seeking.

"Better make it quick," said Desmond, holding his lantern out and squinting through the shadows.

"Got nothin' in here," replied Reese, who decided to partner with him.

In the second car, Houston and Carson had scavenged through the slumps of flour and sugar. They had found a star.

"Bingo!" announced Houston as he placed his lantern by his foot. "Come help me with this."

"Good eye!" Carson replied, and they carried the heavy crate out, brushing their feet through the snow.

Despite the rest fossicking the train, Benny and Al had rounded up three grimy, dusty men, staunchly gripping them by their arms and throwing them into the snow as they begged.

"What's a nigger doin' drivin' a train?" questioned Al, fixing his barrel toward the poor man's forehead.

"They needed people to drive the goods! There were no white folk, so they were desperate!" he cowered under his hands and hung his head low.

"It's only the three of you?" asked Benny, ogling the men.

"Yes, sir!" said another, direly.

"Are you sure? I don't want no unpleasant surprises," Benny spat, like he was growling.

"Yes! Yes, sir! Take my word!" the engineer cried and locked his hands together.

Lugging the fifth crate to the car, Houston approached Benny and whispered, "We can't find the final crate."

"How many we got so far?" Benny asked and turned his

head.

"Five," Houston said, firmly.

The engineer kneeled and said, softly, "Are you wanting those crates with stars?"

"Indeed, we do," said Al, clenching the handle of his revolver tightly.

"Just take them! There were only five," said the dirt-covered engineer, "and we have a list to confirm it, if you're wanting to take a look."

"He's right," said the other cruddy man, "I'm the conductor. I checked and there were only five."

He reached into the pocket of his overalls and snatched a crusty, blackened piece of paper, passing it to Benny.

"Yeah... *Five*. Son of a bitch," he said out loud.

"That'll do," Al confirmed, flicking his hand at the gang and they immediately paraded over to the cars, stocking the crates into the trunks.

"Just one more thing I was gonna ask," Al probed, coughing and stretching his neck, "Why is the train on fire?"

A short flame stuck on the rear of the train, slowly vanishing and leaving behind scorched craters.

"We were attacked," said the engineer, who seemed calmer than before.

"By whom?" pressed Al.

The engineer and conductor looked at one another and then back at the sharply dressed men.

"We don't know exactly, but they was wearing gray and blue suits," the engineer replied.

Al shook. "Peacekeepers?"

"Impossible," Benny stated.

"We can't say, but that's what we thought, too," said the conductor.

The trunks were shut, and the gang had called out to the two.

"Best get goin' before the Peacekeepers show up. They attacked the train, they're pro'ly chasin' it, too," expressed Benny.

"First, we gotta deal with these guys," said Al.

"Wait!" Benny interrupted, jerking his hand forward. Grimacing, he looked at the three dirty men kneeling before him.

"What are you doin'? We'll get rid of 'em now, son," Al imposed in anger.

"No, I got a better solution," said Benny, stepping over to the trembling men. He eyeballed the three and gritted, "Listen to me carefully... Stand up!"

They stood, shaking.

"You know who we are?" Benny questioned.

They shook their heads, slowly.

"Good! Let's keep it that way," Benny nodded and raised his eyebrows. "We were *never* here. Your train was *never* robbed... as far as *you* know. It crashed, and you ran for help. Ya understand?"

They bowed, trying their best not to look at Mister King, but instead stared through Benny's glasses with widened eyes.

"Thank you, kindly," the engineer whimpered, putting his hands together and placed them over his head, "and may God bless you all."

"Go on. Get outta here," stifled Benny, jolting his head at the trees behind them.

They quivered and thanked them, but Al was becoming impatient and stuck out his chest. "Get the fuck outta here!" he snarled, poking out a hand.

In an instant, the grubby men dragged their feet and traveled alongside the tracks, leaving the destroyed train and the gang behind.

"You find anythin' good?" Benny asked, shouting at the others.

"Nothing for us. Unless you're wanting to take coal or rice home, be my guest," Reese chuckled.

"Hey, they got women's clothes if you're interested, Boss," said Houston.

"That's real funny," Al mumbled.

Clusters of snowflakes flurried, dusting their heads and shoulders as they watched the expansive white field begin to dwindle into a scraggy fog. Before the men could slip into their cars, Al spoke out, "Wait. There's somethin' we're gon' wanna check," and the gang froze.

"What now?" sighed Benny.

"Boss, we best move before the Peacekeepers show up," suggested Desmond, opening the trunk.

"I know," said Al calmly, heading toward the car and staring at the crates. "Open it."

It took a few minutes, but with enough yanking and prying, the nails unlatched and the crate was open. And another, too.

"Well, I'll be damned," Benny said quietly.

Chapter Nineteen

The Last Stand

"That son of a bitch!" Al bawled and turned to face the sky, suddenly laughing by himself.

"Christ," gasped Carson, whilst carefully fiddling through the contents of the first large crate, moving bits of dry straw.

"A machine gun?" Desmond stuttered; his mouth wide open, picking up the disassembled parts.

The smaller crates contained mortar rounds which slept on sawdust and straw; four in a box.

"First the dynamite and now mortar rounds," said Reese, stepping away from the cars.

Houston watched from afar and snapped, "That's a bit much... Even for *us*."

Quickly, the crates were tightly closed with old bits of old rope; they decided against hammering them back into place.

"Little bastard coulda blown us up! I told ya," Benny scoffed, veering toward Al. "Galvani can't be trusted."

"You think I don't know that?" Al barked. "I knew he was hidin' somethin' behind that shit-eating fuckin' grin of his!"

"Why'd we do the job, then, Boss?" asked Carson, leaning his arm onto his car. "You didn't think it was risky?"

"Oh, I knew it was *risky*, but I also knew we'd get it done."

"That weren't right, Mister King," said Reese, shaking his head. "Shoulda told us. You, too, Benny. Thought we have this conversation before."

"Hey, don't go blamin' *me*. I was as blind as you!" Benny replied, sulking.

Al eyed the crowd and said, "I wanted to see it for myself. I had no intention of gettin' you all so worked up. It is what it is."

"Now what?" Desmond interrupted. "We take *these* to Lloyd, and we're done?"

Mister King nodded.

"Not a great plan," Houston poked in, wiping his face. "We can't trust the man and you suggest we just hand over these weapons?"

Desmond stood straight, digging his heels into the snow. "What do you suggest? We just walk away?" he said, crossly.

"*That* is a great plan," said Reese, pointing his finger. "We can keep these for ourselves."

"No, we can't," Carson hushed. "They don't belong to us."

"Hey, they don't belong to Lloyd, either," said Benny, switching his rifle to his other arm.

Al raised his voice. "Listen! We're takin' this to Lloyd. The picture's painted, ain't it? Stay focused."

The busted train creaked but stayed upright. It was far too dangerous to be hanging around, thought Mister King, and without spilling a word, he raised his hand with his index finger erect, and created a circular motion with his wrist.

Benny shivered, but it was not the cold or the snow that had shuddered his spine; it was Al's frown. Something felt odd about him, he thought.

They raced down the straight roads with the loot secured, listening to the gravel and snow crunch under their tires. The wipers swept, fighting against the chunky shower of snowflakes, and it was difficult to see through the brimming windscreen. Driving off the slippery path and away from the fields, Benny joined the main road, where the hills began to camber, and twine.

"We're almost there, boys. Don't do anythin' hasty when you see that fucker," said Al, holding onto the door.

"Might wanna repeat that to yourself a few times," said Benny, silently.

"You say somethin'?" Al looked over at him.

"Forget about it."

Crawling behind them at a steady pace, Carson followed, keeping up with Benny by drifting through the snow and ice, and both cars traversed through the center of the road. A final uphill climb was in sight and Benny accelerated hard.

"Jeez! We're lucky. That was a close call," Benny remarked, as his tires squeaked.

They reached the flat and wide cliff top a few miles later, and their hearts pounded. Broader spruce trees separated from the rest, standing by the cliff's edge and sat higher overhead, surrounded by large boulders, small shrubs and dead grass.

A dark figure awaited.

"Must be *him*," hissed Al and perceived the man overlooking the cliff.

The tires inched over the bumps and onto the rocky path leading toward the end of the cliff. Once at a standstill, the engines were cut, and the men withdrew from the black cars, exposing their faces to the bitter cold, and they kept their weapons cradled in their arms.

"'Bout time," Lloyd spat, standing only a few feet away from the gang. "We were gambling on when The Lost Dogs were gon' show up... *Or* if you were going to show up at all."

"Calm down, Mister Gal-" Al paused when something unexpected caught his eye; two pale and blooded bodies hung from the trees with ropes securely fastened around their bruised necks.

"Who were they?" Benny staggered and his mouth remained wide open.

Galvani wore a despicable smile and said, "*Liars,*" before moping. "Anyway... Those *crates,*" he drooled, but the gang was occupied, observing the dangling bodies waver in the wind.

"You're one sick fucker," Benny growled after Lloyd clapped his hands loudly.

"Hey, they had what was coming to them. Lying is not good for business, fellas," Lloyd replied, placing one hand onto his hip and pointing at the gang with the other. "Now. Those *crates*. I will *not* ask again."

The gang exchanged glances at one another.

"I'm waiting," Lloyd buzzed, tiresomely.

As Mister King dipped his head, the men immediately walked to the trunks and retrieved the heavy crates, carrying them to Lloyd and placing them by his feet. Lloyd drew a smile across his face as they delivered more goods to him.

"That all of 'em, Mister Galvani," said Benny, stepping away from the man, who seemed a little concerned.

"Where is the sixth?" Lloyd asked, tensely. He caught a look on Al's face and added, "I told you there were six. Quit fucking around!"

"There weren't six, boy!" Al fumed. "We searched the whole damn train!"

Lloyd paused, calmed himself with a deep breath and put forth, "*All* of it?"

"Yeah... *All* of it. The train's still there if you wanna haul your ass and see for yourself," said Benny.

Scratching his forehead, Lloyd asked, "Is the crew still alive?"

"We killed 'em," said Benny, creasing his eyebrows.

Lloyd looked down at the crates, and everyone remained quiet.

"Mister Galvani," Al broke the stillness, "I had the idea there *was* somethin' you weren't gettin' off ya chest. And now that we're in the midst of all this, ya mind sharin' it with us?"

"About what? What *exactly* are you talking about? 'Cause I ain't got nothing to hide, Mister King. I miscounted the crates. So what?"

"Not *that*!" Benny cackled. "What d'ya plan on doin' with all those explosives?"

With a straight face, Lloyd's eyes hovered over them. "So, I see you took a peek. Should've minded your own business, but I don't blame you. I would've done the same," he said.

"You still haven't answered me, Mister Galvani," Benny taunted, tailoring his rifle in his arms.

"I don't see the need to!" Lloyd growled. "They're in safe hands. I do not plan on using them—not *yet*, at least."

With his fingers, he flicked them rudely toward Al and said, "Step forward, Mister King," to which he obliged, and Lloyd gestured to one of his men, who approached Al with a chunky burlap sack, tossing it at him.

"The payment is all in *here*?" Al queried, ruffling it in his hands and peeping inside.

"Just like I promised," said Lloyd, happily. "If you're willing to count it, be my guest."

Al looked up from under his eyebrows, subtly raised his head and drew a breath. "Thank you," he said, bowing his head.

"Don't get yourself killed, old man," said Lloyd, dully.

With that, Al turned on his heel, pivoting toward the gang and tardily paced. Upon nearing Benny, he came to a halt and swiveled his head to face him. "Exclude the bastard," he whispered.

Benny tilted his head.

Nimbly, the men lifted their firearms and opened fire; abruptly deafening their ears. Bullets ripped through the flesh of Galvani's men and some pierced through their cars. The blunder diminished, leaving the cliff eerily silent after the spent shells clamored the stone beneath them.

"Hold it!" shouted Al, putting up both hands, as he watched Lloyd hunch close to the frozen ground, cowering with his arms behind his head and shutting his eyes.

The gang rushed over, firing at those who survived the hail of bullets. Meanwhile, Al approached Lloyd and fired his revolver into his knee, causing him to tumble onto his back and scream.

"Shoulda killed us when you had the chance! I know you were thinkin' about it, ya bastard," said Al bitterly, towering over him.

Lloyd's hands flew to his wound, and he shrieked, watching his blood gush onto the floor. Shutting his mouth, he breathed heavily through his nose.

"I thought you enjoyed yappin'," Al chuckled. "I like you better this way. I'll be honest."

"Who the fuck do you think you are?" snapped Lloyd.

"Pipe down," Al grouched, shooting him in his other knee and Lloyd clenched his teeth, screeching once more.

"Boss! That's all of 'em!" shouted Benny, walking toward

THOSE LUCKY FELLAS: PART 1

Al. "Let's get outta here while we have the chance."

"What about the bodies?" questioned Desmond.

Carson looked around and suggested, "Desmond's right. We *should* clean up."

"We ain't just leaving it as is?" asked Reese, gesturing with his hand.

"No, it's best if we clear this place and *fast*," said Houston, who squatted by a crate.

Al crouched onto one knee beside Lloyd and said, "Don't worry, you won't die, kid. It's only your knees. And if you want to keep it that way, I suggest you keep your mouth shut." Carefully, he stood and approached the men.

Benny surveyed the crowd. "All right, but let's be quick about it, boys," he said in a hurry.

"Hold on," Al insisted, "Get rid of *everythin'* in sight. We're keepin' the crates. The rest... I'll leave it to you, gentlemen. Have at it."

Whilst the men became occupied, Lloyd's moaning became aggravating and, as a result, Al stomped over to him.

"What the fuck are you waiting for? Kill me, cocksucker!" said Lloyd, ferociously.

Al noticed his behavior change.

"You ain't learnin' if you're dead," Mister King retorted. "I can see it in your eyes, boy. You *ain't* ready to die. Stop tryna to deceive me."

As the bleeding man's unending sniveling and cursing continued, the company heaved the weighty weapons crates and carried them to their cars, lodging them into the trunks. The crimson bodies had been dumped onto the seats of the cars which they arrived in and whatever was left had been crammed into the trunks, too.

"Someone take off the license plates. We're keepin' those, obviously," Benny commanded, and drew closer to Al, who was supervising Lloyd.

"Hurry it up, Mister Falcon," he said.

"I was gon' say the same to you, Boss," Benny supposed and propped up against his car. "Whatever it is you wanna do, you'd best hurry it up *before* the cops or *Peacekeepers* show up. I suggest we kill that son of a bitch and be done for."

"Oh, don't worry, my boy," Al injected, quickly, "I'll finish it... *When you're done*."

At last, Galvani puffed his chest and became mute, despite the pain from his crippled knees. His sudden silence was unusual, Al noticed, and he broke into a laugh.

"What's so damn *funny*?" Al tempted, hovering over him, but Lloyd still wore his silly grin.

"Oh... You... *people* don't understand," he scoffed, glaring at Mister King through narrow eyes and rested on his elbows. "When I am gone... the world will still live on. What did you think was going to happen?" Lloyd sat up, supporting his back with straight elbows and flat palms, and said, "Regardless of what you may do... people, gangs... even the Peacekeepers *will* come for you. Those women and children..." he dipped his head and smiled, "you best keep them safe. Shoulda let me have them... My plans weren't as bad as what's comin' to you fuckers!"

Al crunched his teeth together and removed his revolver from its leather holster, proceeding to point the barrel at Lloyd's sweaty forehead.

"I was plannin' on *not* killin' ya right now, but that mouth is beginnin' to change my mind *real fuckin' fast*," Al lashed out furiously.

Evenly, Lloyd raised his chin, gazed at the sky and said, "Looks like you... fellas had the same idea... as me. To stab one another... in the back. I knew I couldn't trust you. Not many people do. Unfortunately... it looks like you beat me to it."

His groans turned to laughter and back into cries as he watched Benny draw nearer.

"Hurry it up, Mister King!" said Benny, flicking his hand at him.

With a shaking arm, Lloyd pointed at Benny. "Mister Falcon," he panted, "you and I... *We're* the same. *All* of us... are the same. You'll soon come to realize it."

"Enough yappin'!" howled Benny and turned toward his boss. "Get movin', Al. We're almost done," he added, then journeyed to the other men.

The cars rolled over the frosty stone and were parked alongside one another—some faced the cliff with their rear—but the men did not care. What mattered the most was the tidiness of the cliff, and it was indeed *very* tidy.

"Ready to roll, Boss," Benny called, as he briskly waved his arm at Mister King, whose words were on the tip of his tongue just as Lloyd horned in.

"My death will *not* be the last on your list!" he chirped, pointing at Al, "But know this... Your *list* of slaughters *will* keep growing and the Peacekeepers *will* come for you. As will every other gang in Knox... 'cause I fucking ordered it!"

Al recoiled in dread, studying Lloyd from under his cowboy hat. "What?" he blared in a low, soft tone. "What did you say?"

Snickering, Lloyd replied, "Shoulda stayed in retirement! This gang is going to crumble, and you'll see what true failure looks like!"

Immediately, Al holstered his revolver and snagged Lloyd by the hair, forcibly turning him around and tightly pinning his forearm under his chin. Lying on his stomach, Lloyd attempted to slither out, but his legs were too injured to move.

"*This* is what failure looks like!" Al flared, towing Lloyd's hair to lift his head.

Al flashed a wink at Benny, who commenced the final part of the cleanup; the tattered cars were propelled forward and rolled off the edge, colliding against the huge rocks and smashing into the waves beneath them.

"You think you've already won?" Lloyd spouted, and his breathing became uneven.

Releasing his arm, Al threw him onto the ground and reverted him onto his back once more and for the final time.

"Your points are weak, and so are you," he said, digging his knee into Lloyd's stomach and punching his face; pummeling his jaw and nose before viciously beating the sides of his face. No matter how much blood gushed from his split cheek, mouth and nostrils, the endless beating continued, and the thudding was not going to end soon.

"Boss!" Benny thundered, worryingly, dashing over to Al, who was hammering into a bloodied mess. "Mister King, that's enough!" he grumbled, but Al continued.

"Get off me!" trilled Al, pushing away Benny's arms, and he did not notice it was him.

"Knock it off, Al, he's dead!" replied Benny, pulling him off Lloyd's body.

THOSE LUCKY FELLAS: PART 1

Both men looked at one another blankly.

"Fuckin' Christ... I don't know came over me, son," Al mumbled, breathing deeply.

"Fuck... Al, what did you do?"

The men stormed over and goggled at the two.

"Our job here is *done*, boys," said Al, raising himself.

The stillness was unnerving.

"Get rid of the body. Throw it off the cliff," said Benny and he stood up, too. "And when you're done... we're goin' home."

Al held out a bloodied hand and thought patiently.

"Benny..." he said, giving a sidelong glance, "we've gotta head somewhere. *Right now.*"

Promptly, Mister Galvani's body was swung and thrown over the cliffside, too, splashing faintly when it crashed into the sea.

"Gentlemen, head home," announced Benny, scanning the floor for anything they may have missed. "Me and Mister King are headin' somewhere, but expect us to join you shortly."

"See you at the house," added Al, and bowed at the men as they invaded Houston's car.

The men nodded back firmly.

"So... Where are we headed? Shouldn't we be runnin' home with the rest?" Benny proposed, wrapping up his rifle with his arms.

"I got a theory I wanna test," Al remarked and wiped the warm blood from his hands with his handkerchief. "I *need* you to back me up, Benny."

"Sure—as long as you don't get us both killed, I'm fine with that," he said, ogling Al's messy hands.

"Get in the car, Mister Falcon."

Together, without delay, Benny and Al hopped into the Hudson Hornet and the engine purred, smoking in the cold.

"Where're we goin'? And are you *sure* this is a good idea?" Benny put forth, stowing his rifle onto the back seat.

"Trust me, son, there's somethin' we have *got* to see," Al said, lowering his voice as he spoke. "You remember Galvani's house?"

Benny affirmed.

"Good. Take us there."

Chapter Twenty

A Smoking Gun

The journey across the white mountain roads was comfortable, now that the job was over, thought Benny, as he drove over the sweeping hills and past the slender spruce trees, where the snow became slushy, and the snowfall tapered. As they crested a hill, they caught a glimpse of the valley below; a glittering expanse of lights in the darkness.

"We have no business with Galvani. He *is* dead, after all. So, what're we doin'? Finishin' off the rest of the family?" Benny pressed, gazing at the murky road ahead.

"There's somethin' I wanted to see. You'll understand when we're there," said Al, propping his head against the seat's warm leather.

"This better not be a waste of a trip," Benny mumbled and scratched his lip.

"I hope I'm right about this," said Al, and followed the horizon with his eye.

Soon after, they approached a small town. The tires, digging through wet snow, rolled through the deserted streets. The streetlights emanated a soft glow over the snow-covered buildings and sidewalks, casting long shadows. Besides a lone figure passing by a parked car, the town seemed empty. They neared the outskirts of the curious town, and the streetlights grew fewer and far between, urging the night to grow.

"Take the next left and follow those trees," Al denoted, pointing ahead.

Still travelling, the road stretched into flat, open fields and the last of the trees receded behind them, replaced by vast plains.

"I'd hate livin' this far out," Benny mentioned, observing the surrounding greenery. "There's *nothin'* out here. What's a man gon' do? Lloyd ain't even a farmer."

"That's the point," Al chortled. "There is *nothin'* out here. He likes to hide, so I'd say he picked the perfect spot... If you ask me."

Benny turned the wheel.

"Easy on the gas, son," said Al, holding onto the door and sitting up.

"I wanna get home *fast*. I want this whole damn thing to be *over*, Mister King," said Benny.

"So do I, but we ain't gonna do anythin' if you get us killed, now will we?"

Ahead, a little farmhouse propped at the end of an expansive field with only a tall windmill for company and Benny drove prudently over the beaten path, hitting the brake as they converged.

Benny sighed and muttered, "Not *another* farmhouse."

"Stop *here*," Al put forth, lifting his left hand.

"We're burnin' this one, too?" Benny laughed and parked beside a white fence.

"Shut up and get out, Mister Falcon."

The engine slept, and they left the warmth of the Hudson Hornet, welcomed by the chilling breeze of the wintry night.

"Why'd you stop me so *far away*?" Benny asked, curiously, and pointed at the farmhouse ahead of them. "That's at least fifty yards, man."

"Pay attention," Al disrupted. "I got a bad feelin' about all of this."

"So, if we ain't here to finish the rest of 'em, then what are we here for?" said Benny grumpily.

"Keep an eye on the house," Al replied and pushed himself closer to the car, resting his hand on the roof. "The lights are on, and the cars seem... Hold on."

He stood upright.

"What about those cars?" asked Benny, alertly peering at the house, too.

"Peacekeepers," Al whispered, and his lips parted.

To their surprise, their composure was shattered by a re-verberating echo emanating from the farmhouse and the sharp sound tore across the fields, dwindling as it reached them.

"Gunshots? Peacekeepers went after them, too?" Benny yelled and pivoted his head to watch Al storm across the path.

"I knew they'd show up. I wanted to see it for myself. Let's go, Mister Falcon."

Quickly, Benny sprinted behind him and caught hold of his shoulder, pulling forcefully until he spun around to face him.

"What're ya doin', Benny?" Al spat. "We got the chance to kill 'em both!"

"I would have turned the car around if you told me earlier. We ain't goin' in there to fight a fuckin' family and those god-damn Peacekeepers. Not the two of us," said Benny, sturdily.

"Vulpes is pro'ly in there, too! We can finish off all those fuckers!" said Al, jerking his shoulder away from Benny's fist.

"Boss, we'll get our chance when the time comes. This is a *bad* plan," Benny retorted, putting out his hand. "If we take out Galvani's family *and* the Peacekeepers, people will know a third party got involved and if they realize it was The Lost Dogs, things'll go south for us real fast. Remember what Lloyd said?"

Regardless of Benny towering over him, Al stormed forward and said, "I am *not* losin' this chance."

"Don't do it, Al," said Benny, speaking quietly and sticking out his palm. "Listen to me, Boss. This fight don't belong to us. If we kill Vulpes now, we'll have to fight the rest of 'em and we are *not* ready."

Lazily, Al's eye shifted from the farmhouse to Benny's pale face, just as the sharp echoes from across the fields faded into silence.

"Benny," Al heaved a sigh, "you're one stubborn bastard. I guess we're goin' home if that's what you believe in. Maybe you're right—for now—but when our chance does come, you ain't stoppin' me."

"Of course. Hell, I'll be sure to throw you into the action myself," Benny laughed and reached into his pocket for a cigar, but it was empty. "Goddamnit," he said, faintly.

Al jounced his head heavily and said, "All right, I'm sorry. Let's head home before somethin' gets outta hand."

Benny pointed at Al and said, "See, *that* is a great plan, Boss."

"Shut up and get in the car, would ya?" Al said under his breath and flounced back to the car, snatching the door handle.

Together, in a swift motion, they slid onto the plush seat of the Hudson Hornet and Benny gripped the steering wheel. With a twist of the silver key, the engine roared, and the vibrations coursed through the car. Benny pressed his foot against the accelerator and turned the car around, then propelled it forward with an exhilarating surge of speed; a trail of dust danced behind.

"Boss, this night was... It was a *strange* night, no doubt," said Benny, combing his silky hair with his fingers. "It was not what I expected."

"Me neither, Benny, but we got to live in the end, right?" said Al, eyeing him.

As they embarked toward the manor, returning to their cozy and peaceful home, Benny realized that the journey would be miserable, so he remained quiet. Al did, too, surprisingly.

The engine's low rumble strained the silence which filled the car. Both men had their bodies subtly angled away from one another, as if seeking comfort in the corners of their respective seats. The passing hills and trees offered fleeting distractions, and each mile seemed to be stretched longer than when they had first come.

"Radio should kill time," said Al, softly, beginning to feel weary.

He stretched out his fingers and, after missing a few times, he succeeded in twisting the knob until a muffled melody began to chime, causing them both to be lost in their own thoughts.

Drowsily, Al glared out of the steamy window and counted the few glittery stars overhead. He removed his hat and placed it on the seat beside him. His eye grew heavy, eventually surrendering to the exhaustion that enticed.

"Good riddance," Benny whispered, peeking over to Al and smiling as he slumbered.

Driving past the strange town and through the twisty moonlit roads, Benny eased off the gas, allowing the Hudson

Hornet to sweep over the steep, wavy hills.

He traveled steadily, ignoring the derailed train to his left, of course, and bowled on through Silver Springs; an eerie memory filled his mind when he watched the docks by the beautiful, gleaming lake.

Finally, the long bridge out of the unusual little town was in sight, widening as it hung over the river beneath. Benny accelerated a little harder, allowing the car to sing, like a morning bird.

As the mountains dissolved into the distance, Valport's pine trees emerged. Bathed in the elegant glow of the moonlight, the quiet streets of the town slept; shop lights were dimmed, and streetlights flickered through the frigid night. The cold air seeped over the buildings, casting frost on the rooftops and windows, making them shimmer under the clear, moonlit sky.

Benny nudged Al, who snored in short bursts. "Wake up, Boss," he said, "we're almost home."

Al grunted, lifted his head, and said, "Shoulda woke me up *when* we arrived outside our doors."

"Best part is when you wake up *before* gettin' home. It don't feel the same when you get there first," said Benny, calmly.

Al shivered and rubbed his hands together.

"You cold, Mister King?" Benny asked, smiling from one side of his mouth. "It ain't even cold."

"No, I just feel *real* good," said Al, happily. "You know the feelin'... When you finish a long job. Haven't done somethin' like this in... in *years*, so it's—"

"Yeah, I understand," Benny chimed in. "The feelin' that you're lucky to be alive? Yeah, I know *that* feelin', Mister King."

THOSE LUCKY FELLAS: PART 1

The final stretch of bumpy road lay ahead; smothered in thick lumps of dirt and the headlights forged pools of warm flares, guiding their way through the blackness and through the silhouettes.

"We made it," announced Al, holding onto the door as they glided over the road. "I hope the men are all right. I hope they aren't worried 'bout us."

Benny chuckled and said, "You should be more frightened about Caroline not wantin' to beat us for takin' so long. And the men... God, I hope they kept quiet about our little trip."

When the scent of home filled the car, Al put up his hand, causing Benny to become startled.

"What is it, old man?" he announced.

"Start slowin' down. There's somethin' I want to ask, and I don't want to be sayin' what I'm about to say in front of the rest," declared Al, moving his eyepatch.

"And what did you wanna ask?" said Benny and slowly moved his foot from the gas pedal to the brake.

When Mister King felt the car slowing down, he coughed into his fist and asked, "Any idea what we'll be doin' with the weapons? We sure as hell ain't keepin' it in the house."

"I thought you might say that, so I already did some plannin'," Benny retorted. "Remember Caesar?"

"You talked?"

Benny nodded his head and said, "Before this train job, he wanted to see me. Said he had somethin' important he wanted to discuss with me. Turns out, we can hand the weapons over to him!"

Quickly, Al leaned forward and put forth, "He knew about the job?"

"See, that's what I was wonderin', too!" Benny laughed. "I had the same thought process, but it is Caesar, after all. I hope you ain't disappointed in me, Boss."

"No, Benny, 'course not. We got the upper hand thanks to you. And Caesar, obviously," Al replied, spinning his ring around his wrinkled finger.

The house was up ahead, and Benny pulled into the driveway, following the path leading into the great yard. He parked by the fountain.

"Always parkin' by the fountain, aren't ya, Benny?" Al laughed and his excitement was noticeable.

"Yes, sir!" he shouted ardently, then bailed from the car, locking the door behind him.

As one, their steps synchronized as they traversed the weathered stone path and stumbled before the pretty, welcoming front doors of the manor; a sight which Benny thought he would never miss so dearly, except for one undeniable obstacle hindering their path—the aggravating presence of Caroline.

What could she possibly want?

"You're both *late*. Where'd the two of you run off to?" she probed, and her words felt as though they were drilling the men's ears.

"We did a small job we didn't want the others to get involved in, so it don't concern you, either, Caroline," said Benny, firmly, fixing his tie and removing his leather gloves.

Caroline, with a quick glance, looked at the two tired men before her and said, "Fine. Just hurry up inside because you're both late for dinner... again."

"Darling, come on, let's go eat. Everything went smoothly," Al added and eyeballed Benny. "Right, Mister Falcon?"

THOSE LUCKY FELLAS: PART 1

"Sure! 'Course it did," Benny replied, smiling at Missus King. "Your husband should join us in more jobs. He *sure* knows how to make things go *smoothly*. Ain't that right, Boss?"

"What happened out there?" Caroline asked and her brown eyes widened.

"Nothin'," Al said, slowly.

He put his arm around his wife's waist and the three walked inside, where Sloane welcomed them.

"Welcome home!" her delicate voice echoed.

"It's good to see ya, Sloane. Felt like I had gone for a long time," Benny acknowledged and tilted his head at her.

"We're having roast chicken tonight. Now, go and get ready for dinner," she replied eagerly, pointing toward the stairs in the great hall.

"Yes, ma'am!" he said.

"Al, darling, you go on ahead, too. I'll see you at the table. And don't be late. Both of you!" stated Caroline and kissed her husband on his cold cheek.

The soothing spray of hot water dripped down Benny's weary body as the droplets danced on his skin and relaxed his muscles. A gentle mist enveloped the bathroom and the scent of coconut and honey filled the air, all while Benny soaked in himself under the water.

Feeling refreshed, he slipped into his dark red, woolly bathrobe and shaved his neck and chin with a sharp razor. His hair and friendly mutton chops were oiled, too, and he sprayed cologne against his skin, stinging where the razor had met him.

"Uncle Benny! Dinner is ready!" a young voice called from outside his bedroom door, followed by more tapping.

Benny opened the door carefully, lifted the joyful girl and

said, "Is that right, little miss? Well, let's go and eat!"

"I can walk!" she called, gleefully, whilst being held in Benny's arms.

"I know you can, but you always misbehave," said Benny, chuckling. "All you kids are naughty."

A wonderful and scrumptious scent filled the halls and strengthened as the two approached the grand staircase.

"They made a lot of food tonight," said the young girl.

"Oh, is that right? Good! I'm *starvin*'," Benny announced, licking his dry bottom lip.

Soon, they entered the cozy dining room, where the girl had run toward Sloane, who told her to sit quietly. Benny perched beside Al and watched the candles in the center flicker; relaxing his mind and ignoring the soft chatter from the rest.

"We ain't eaten all day," Benny whispered to Al, who examined his fork.

"Now that I think about it, I could pro'ly eat more than you, Mister Falcon," he replied with a smile.

"Don't start," said Caroline, carrying a large golden-brown roasted chicken and placing it in front of Al.

A tasty aroma veiled the air when two more roasted chickens, bowls of steaming mashed potatoes and a few gravy boats had been brought out and had scattered the table, all of which were prepared by the ladies.

"We thought you gentlemen were going out for a while, so we ladies thought you'd be starving when you get back," Caroline announced, taking a seat beside her husband.

"Thank you, ladies. You've outdone yourselves yet again!" said Al.

THOSE LUCKY FELLAS: PART 1

With a knife in his hand, Al carved the tender meat and its succulent juices dripped when he placed it onto his plate. Mashed potatoes and chopped carrots accompanied the meat, and bottles of white wine were shared amongst the men and women.

"This is *delicious*, ladies!" Benny expressed, washing down the dinner with his ice-cold whiskey.

"Thank you, Mister Falcon," said Valentine, who smiled at him.

"I knew it was *you* who'd cooked it," Benny added, ripping apart the meat and dipping it into the thick gravy.

"Actually, it was *me*," Sloane interrupted before giggling.

The men looked at one another blankly.

"No, it was *me*," said Caroline. "The dinner was *my* idea."

Benny leaned over to Al and whispered, "You know, maybe the train wasn't so bad."

Al nodded as Benny moved away.

Once the dinner had concluded, they brought out the dessert; soft chocolate mousse and it filled the room with a sweet, sticky scent.

"Kids'll enjoy it, but I ain't havin' *that*," said Benny.

"Try it, man," said Reese, digging his spoon into the wobbly dessert.

"It tastes pretty great," Desmond expressed.

"No, no. It's not my thing."

Al swiftly cleared his plate and mentioned, "You're missin' out, Benny."

"Christ," he mumbled, ogling Al's chocolate-stained teeth.

"We just have one more meetin', fellas. Somethin' crossed my mind earlier and I feel like it's right to... *discuss* it with ya,"

Al claimed, while the ladies cleared the table and the children began to run around the hallway and into the living room.

The men bowed their heads.

"Meet me upstairs in a couple of minutes, gentlemen," he said and with that, he departed from the table.

"What do you think he wants?" asked Carson, slowly.

"I hope it's not *another* job. We *just* did one." Houston answered.

"The way I see it, he's pro'ly got somethin' to complain about, like he always does," Benny remarked, feeling peeved.

In no time, the men scurried up the grand staircase and their heels walloped against the white carpet as they stampeded through the door, where Al stood and drew the brown and white floral curtains.

"Take a seat, gentlemen. This shouldn't take long... I hope."

Together, the chairs were plucked from the lengthy table; their collective movements accompanied by faint squeaks, and they all landed upon the cushioned seats before glancing at Al, who still stood and hovered over them.

"Let us begin," Al announced, turning around from the window and stepping toward the table. "A job well done, fellas! But let's cut through the bullshit."

"Oh, here we go," mumbled Benny.

"The train job we did for Mister Galvani didn't go *fully* accordin' to plan, let's be honest," stated Al, cracking his knuckles and his eye hopped from one man to the next.

"I wonder *why* it didn't," Benny chuckled, wiping his glasses on his sleeve.

"Save it, Mister Falcon," urged Al grumpily. "In the end, *we* were the ones on top, so let's keep it that way. So here is what

I am proposin'. What Galvani said about us *may* be true and all, but from here on out, we're only workin' with people I... *we* trust. That means we're doin' things *our* way."

Confused, the men stared at one another before Benny stated, "I thought we was retired, Boss. You ever gave that *any* thought?"

"Listen... If things change—which sometimes happens—Lloyd is just the first example of what's to come *if* we get stabbed in the back," Mister King indicated, "but that ain't gon' happen. And one more thing. I know I said we're retired, which is why we're *only* doin' jobs that land on *our* doorstep," Al declared. "No more chasin' butterflies."

"So, after all of *that*, we're not *really* retired?" Houston asked, wiping his palm across his face. "Fine. I guess it's like retirement."

"I can live with that, so long as we're not causing trouble for the women and children," Desmond expressed, leaning back into his chair.

Al closed his eye and bobbed his head. "What about the rest of you?"

"I suppose that *is* better than fightin' for fuckin' nothin'," Carson disclosed. "Less worry for us."

"Sounds like a decent idea," Reese proposed. "In fact, *that* plan is way better than this whole damn train stunt we pulled."

They all eyed Benny, who began scratching his forehead.

"Looks like I ain't got much of a choice, but if it works, then I'm a happy man," he put forth, gliding his fingers through his hair.

"Very well. It's settled," said Al, proudly. "Oh, and the weapons we stole... Benny, do me a favor, would ya?"

"Take 'em to Caesar tomorrow?" Benny sighed loudly, sticking up his hand.

"Perfect! I'll leave you to it. Thank you, Mister Falcon," Al laughed, leaving the room, snappily.

Benny and the others remained in the comfy room, gibbering amongst themselves, attempting to forget about the meeting entirely.

Suddenly, Caroline knocked on the door in little bursts and turned her head around the corner. "It's late, gentlemen. Go to sleep," she insisted, making little noise.

"You fellas go on ahead. I've got some... *thinkin'* to do," said Benny, watching them vacate the room.

The room was dimly lit by a single lamp flickering in the corner, casting a glow over the white wallpaper. Benny buried his head into his hands and thought, but he failed to focus his mind on anything. Instead, he massaged his forehead with his fingertips.

"Guess I'm too tired," he whispered to himself.

Photographs of the children adorned the walls and aged books sat on the bookshelf, covered in a thin layer of dust. He watched the stunning grandfather clock, stared at the white ceiling and played with his silver glasses, yet his mind felt empty.

It was as if time stood still.

Chapter Twenty-One

Sit and Dream

June had arrived and its bright blue sky made way for the scorching sun, drenching the early afternoon in a golden glow. Orange daylilies blossomed and the spruce trees gave way to vivid green needles.

"It's 'bout time we got some heat in Knox, but I miss the cold," said Benny, exhaustedly. "It's too goddamn hot."

"Why don't you give the barbecue a rest and go sit indoors, Benny? It's cooler inside," Sloane giggled, opening the cap of an ice-cold Narragansett Lager and handing it to him.

"The kids want more hot dogs, and this barbecue ain't gonna cook food itself," he replied, smiling and rolling up the sleeves of his white buttoned shirt before taking the slippery bottle.

Sloane smiled and tapped his shoulder. "That's just your excuse for not letting anyone else use it, Mister Falcon."

"Well, the summer *does* make every man the best chef," he laughed, wiping the sweat from his forehead with his wrist and gulping down the crispy, golden beer.

The children's playful giggles echoed as they chased each other around the yard, spraying one another with cold water from a hose. Sausages grilled over the coal, sizzling beside the beef burgers and slices of tomatoes, onions and cucumber roasted, too.

"Damn, I *could* have another, but I'm tryna keep my gut healthy," said Al, patting his belly and hovering over to him.

"I'll make you another one, Boss," said Benny joyfully.

"What happened? Missus King ain't lettin' ya have another bite? That's a shame."

"That's funny. An old man can't look after his own gut?" Al retorted, placing his empty beer bottle on a red and white checkered picnic table. "You'll understand in a couple years. I'll leave you to it, son. Don't go burnin' yourself," Al stated, grinning and walking over to Missus King.

In a whisper, Benny chortled.

"Here are the plates," said Valentine, happily, as she placed a stack of white dinner plates onto the table and removed the empty beer bottle.

"Thank you, Valentine. Could you do me a favor and call the kids, please?" Benny put forth, building the hot dogs and beef burgers and stacking them onto the plates.

"Of course," she replied and clapped her hands, calling out in her soft, calming voice.

The sounds of a distant radio became muffled when the children dashed over to the picnic table.

"Kids, be careful! It's hot!" shouted Benny, waving the curls of smoke with his hand.

"Sit still!" yelled Valentine.

"Not a word out of any of you!" hailed Sloane.

With that, the children came to a halt, settling into silence and their lips sealed tight, afraid to utter another word, while the cheerful music was heard once again.

"That made 'em shut up," Benny laughed, taking another sip of his beer and playing with the greasy spatula. "Thank God it was not Caroline. She would've eaten all you kids alive."

"I *can* hear you, Benny," Caroline called out from under the shade, resting with the other women.

THOSE LUCKY FELLAS: PART 1

Before long, the picnic table became a palette of colors, decorated with rich salads and chopped pickles. Colorful ceramic bowls brimmed with sliced tomatoes, crisp lettuce, chopped onions and grated cheese, complemented with a bottle of ketchup, of course. Freezing Coca-Cola bottles were served to the children, too.

Painting the sky with a blanket of pink and orange, the sun set over the horizon, widening the shadows and allowing the cool breeze to liberate. The last rays of sunlight danced upon the manor's cream walls.

"Mister Falcon," Sloane spoke tenderly, "why don't you take a seat? You've been standing by that barbecue *all* day."

"Today went pretty fast. We all had fun! *That's* what matters," said Benny mirthfully.

"That's no excuse to be standing over there, Mister Falcon," Valentine chipped in, tidying the long picnic table.

Both ladies giggled.

"Hey, a *man's* gotta work the grill and I'm the best man for it," informed Benny. "What more can I say? I'm an honest man."

Without hurrying, Mister King stepped outside and flagged with an outstretched arm and howled, "Mister Falcon, come on over here... if you don't mind! I got somethin' you won't wanna miss!"

"Jeez, your grandfather is gon' give himself a stroke someday," Benny uttered, raising his eyebrows at Sloane.

He walked over to Al, stomping through the dry yard, and said, "What's the hurry? This better be good."

"Oh, don't worry, my boy," Al responded, and wore an enormous smile from ear to ear. "I told the rest of 'em to join me upstairs once they're free."

"And?"

"And we're waitin' on you, Benny!" said Mister King, pivoting and hopping along the path into the manor's great hallway.

A few minutes had slipped away before Benny reached the room upstairs, greeted by the rest when he entered.

"So, what's this fuss about?" he asked politely, lighting his favorite cigar.

"Been some time since we worked, hasn't it?" Al mentioned, directed Benny to a chair with his arm. "Take a seat and the rest of you get comfortable."

"We're workin' again?" Benny inquired, holding his vanilla-scented cigar between his index finger and thumb and rested on the comfy chair.

"I hope the job landed on *our* doorstep this time, Boss," said Houston.

"It did."

"Did it *really*?" Reese probed, leaning forward.

"Yes."

"I'll take your word for it, Boss," stated Desmond, pointing a finger at Al.

"Good."

"Last jobs we did were a little odd," Carson expressed, resting both hands on the table.

"Hear me out."

"We're workin' in the summer, ain't we?" Benny sighed.

"Goddamnit," mumbled Al. "Can't you just *listen* to what I have to say?"

Benny pointed at a large tape recorder that lay in the center of the table. "You sure you know how to work that thing?"

"It's not hard, man," Al replied, unbuttoning his top button on his white shirt. "Take a listen to this, fellas. I've already heard what's on there, but you're gonna thank me later. Tape was delivered this mornin'."

"Oh, this is gonna be *good* if Mister King is gettin' all *excited*," Benny declared, savoring the sweet smoke in his mouth.

"Are you finished?"

Benny tilted his head.

"Right, gentlemen. We can begin."

With his middle finger, Al pressed the black play button, and the tapes started to spin.

The room reverberated a blithesome, seasoned voice of a man which filled the space with its jovial resonance.

"*Good morning, or afternoon, gentlemen! My name is Clyde Marlowe. You may or may not have heard of me, but I heard The Lost Dogs are back in business. I've been hearing some great things about you fellas. That pleases me because I have a pretty big job for you. Now, I know you won't refuse this offer, which is why I am proposing it to you to begin with. We'll both be working together very closely, so keep this between us. Anyway, take a seat. This may come as a surprise, but you'll want to hear this.*"

Within a few minutes, the tape endlessly spun and the crumbly voice had expired; a series of cadenced clicks ensued.

"We're *really* goin' through with that job, ain't we?" Benny pondered, disposing his cigar into an ashtray.

"Oh, we will be, gentlemen! We *sure* as hell will be," Al brimmed with excitement. "Better prepare yourselves for this one, boys, 'cause this is gon' be a *big* one."

About the Author

Born in the UK and intrigued by America's noir culture, Awais Aftab Khan spent a few years experimenting with characters, worlds and plots before he began writing Those Lucky Fellas, a novel he was eager to bring to life.

While studying the art of filmmaking, Awais continued to hone his storytelling skills and he spent countless hours crafting complex characters, intricate plots and an immersive world, all while striving to capture the essence of the noir genre he loved.

Now, with Those Lucky Fellas completed, Awais is excited to share his vision with the rest of the world. He hopes readers will be drawn into the gritty, atmospheric world he's created and will connect with the unforgettable characters he's brought to life.

Milton Keynes UK
Ingram Content Group UK Ltd.
UKHW041922310823
427823UK00001B/13

9 798223 103851